THE SECRET SUNSHINE PROJECT

BENJAMIN DEAN

illustrated by SANDHYA PRABHAT

SIMON & SCHUSTER

First published in Great Britain in 2022 by Simon & Schuster UK Ltd

1 3 5 7 9 10 8 6 4 2

Simon & Schuster UK Ltd
1st Floor, 222 Gray's Inn Road
London WC1X 8HB

www.simonandschuster.co.uk
www.simonandschuster.com.au
www.simonandschuster.co.in

Simon & Schuster Australia, Sydney
Simon & Schuster India, New Delhi

A CIP catalogue record for this book
is available from the British Library.

PB ISBN 978-1-4711-9975-2
eBook ISBN 978-1-4711-9976-9
eAudio ISBN 978-1-3985-0717-3

Typeset in Garamond by M Rules
Printed and bound by CPI Group (UK) Ltd, Croydon, CR0 4YY

*To Mum, Gran and Ellie, for always
bringing sunshine to my life.*

CHAPTER 1

THE COLOURS AT THE END OF THE RAINBOW

So, before we get into this, there's one important thing I should tell you – I've been to the end of the rainbow. Okay, yeah, I know that sounds pretty unbelievable and you don't have any reason to trust me just yet, but it's true! Sure, according to scientists and, you know, clever people, the end of the rainbow doesn't *actually* exist. Everybody knows that, right? We've all tried searching for that magical pot of gold, but no matter how fast you run towards it, the rainbow never seems to get any closer. Apparently it's nothing more than an optical illusion, something that doesn't really exist at all.

Except it does. I know the end of the rainbow exists because I've been there myself and I didn't even have to go that far to find it – it was just a quick trip on the Victoria line tube into central London. I don't think the scientists thought to look for it there, but it was right under their noses all along.

In fact, the end of the rainbow is all over the world, in little pockets of colour that appear for short periods of time, once a year, before they vanish again. People in the know travel to these special spots and celebrate their discovery with each other. It's a happy place. A place to feel safe and sound, and where you can somehow feel both ordinary and extraordinary at the same time.

Okay, I'm going to stop calling it the end of the rainbow and call it by its actual name now, so things don't get too confusing. This place is called Pride. I don't want to be biased, but Pride might just be my favourite place in the world (and I say that as someone who once went to Thorpe Park four times in a summer holiday). You see, Pride has a magic to it, something that you can't really explain or describe but that you need to *feel* to really understand it. Sure, that magic can't last for ever – I know that now after everything – but, even for just a moment, Pride can make people feel like they're not alone in the world.

My older sister, Riley, was one of those people. She's sixteen years old now but she knew she liked girls way before then. She didn't tell anyone, though – she kept it a secret. I'd noticed something was up – she's my big sister, and it's basically my job to notice. It wasn't like she was in a bad mood or anything; more that she just retreated into herself, like she was trying to keep something from us. If we asked what was wrong, Riley would shrug and mumble that it was nothing, or worse, she'd snap and tell us to leave her alone. But, when she was ready, she opened the door and let us inside.

'I think I like girls,' Riley blurted out over the dinner table one night. Her eyes widened as the words escaped out into the open, floating just out of reach so that they couldn't be taken back.

Mum and Dad looked surprised, but I think that was only because we'd been talking about how Mr Eddington at number seventy-two had started opening his curtains in just his underpants, and Mum was wondering how best to tell him to, you know, stop doing that.

'It's nothing to be embarrassed about, honey,' Mum said, reaching for Riley's hand, all thoughts of Mr Eddington and his underpants forgotten.

'Nothing at all,' Dad added, always Mum's sidekick. 'It doesn't make you any different from anybody else.'

Mum mulled something over in the brief silence. I didn't really know what I was meant to do in this situation, so I took the opportunity to nab the last roast potato from the middle of the table. I was fighting a battle with the ketchup lid (don't frown – dipping roast potatoes in ketchup is the *only* way to eat them) when Mum turned to me.

'Bea, will you give us a minute?' she asked carefully. I thought that was unfair considering I hadn't finished my dinner yet, and also because I didn't want to be left out of the adults' conversation. Riley wasn't even technically an adult either!

I grumped and sulked and ended up sitting in the nook under the stairs, listening in to the hushed conversation going on without me. I didn't really know what any of it meant. All I gathered was that Riley had a crush on a girl at school and Mum said it was a good thing that she felt comfortable enough to get it off her chest and talk to them about it. Mum's always made it clear that we can talk to her and Dad about anything (although this wasn't strictly true because when I confessed that it was me who replaced the sugar with the salt, I got grounded for a week).

Once Riley had shaken the secret off, she was a lot more like herself. Nobody really talked about it for a week or so after, and to be honest, I'd forgotten all about it until Mum and Dad called us downstairs for A Talk. Those kinds of talks, where we'd find Mum and Dad at the kitchen table, were never good news. It was usually along the lines of, 'We're spring-cleaning the whole house this weekend so don't make any plans,' or something just as terrible. But this time it was different. They were sitting in the kitchen, a laptop between them, and that's when they told us about London Pride.

'We've been thinking about what you told us the other night and if there's anything we can do to make you feel comfortable,' Mum said to Riley. 'I can't believe we didn't think of it straight away – Rue talks non-stop about it every summer, and it just hit me that it's right on our doorstep. In fact, the next one is in two weeks' time!'

She picked up the laptop and spun it round so we could see what she was talking about. At the top of the screen were the words 'LONDON LGBTQ+ PRIDE' in colourful bubble writing, and below were a ton of pictures bordered with rainbows and explosions of confetti. It was London as I'd never seen it before, brimming with colour like one of Mum's paintings.

'What is it?' I asked, my eyes feasting on the pictures.

'It's a sort of parade, I suppose, with marching and floats and music,' Dad said, his own dark eyes lighting up. I just knew he was thinking about embarrassing us with his dance moves. Even though he was somewhat unco-ordinated, Dad loved to dance. It made Mum laugh. It made me and Riley groan.

Mum nodded. 'Rue and Travis go every year. They love it.' Rue was Mum's best friend from university, Travis was his husband, and I'd basically known them both for my entire life. The three of them were 'thick as thieves' according to Dad. They shared an art studio where they painted and gossiped, but Travis always said Mum and Rue did more of one than the other.

'What's LGBTQ?' I thought out loud, reading the bubble writing on the laptop screen and eyeing a picture of a woman who had decorated her wheelchair with rainbow-coloured streamers. She was waving a flag above her head and laughing.

'Lesbian, gay, bisexual, transgender and queer,' Mum reeled off without hesitation. 'Rue and Travis, for example – they're gay and so they're a part of that community. And now your sister is too.' Mum gave Riley a squeeze and a smile. 'So, that's why I thought we could go.'

Riley's mouth dropped open slightly. 'We're going to Pride?' she half-whispered.

Dad grinned. 'Yep. We figured it'd be good for you to be around other people who are a part of this community too. It looks like it'll be a great day out for us all.' He paused as he caught the expression on Riley's face, which was frozen between more than one emotion. 'That's if you want to go ...'

Without another word, Riley shot up and wrapped her arms around Mum and Dad with a squeal. 'Of *course* I want to go!'

And so it was settled. On a sunny weekend in July, we woke up early, put on something bright – I wore a T-shirt that said 'My sister's gay, get over it' (a gift from Rue) – and jumped on the tube into central London. It was a day I'll never forget, mostly because Riley insisted on snapping pictures of literally everything. From the moment we arrived, there were crowds of people everywhere, dressed in every colour of the rainbow and wearing enough glitter and sparkle to cover all the pavements in the city. There were stalls selling rainbow flags and obviously there was lots of music too, with dancers and singers celebrating around every street corner. And, of course, there was the parade itself.

We managed to squeeze ourselves up against the barrier, penned in on all sides by people with smiles plastered on their faces as they craned their necks to catch glimpses of the floats and trucks sliding slowly past, with music blasting out and dancers twirling on board. On one float, a bunch of people wearing elaborate feathers that reached high above their heads blew whistles and danced in perfect unison. For a brief second, I thought I saw a kid, no older than me, in the middle of it all, his glasses perched on the end of his nose and a look of bewilderment etched on his face as he tried to keep up with the dance moves. But the feathers soon hid him from sight and I started to think it must've just been my imagination.

Each float was somehow more majestic than the last. Mum couldn't stop oohing and aahing at every wonder that passed by, and I knew she was taking mental notes for a new painting when we got home. Dad, meanwhile, was particularly interested in a group of people wearing wigs which towered above their heads like a tiered cake. Their faces looked like Mum had painted them with one of her brushes, colour sweeping across cheekbones and eyelids in a flourish. Of course, as soon as Dad saw them dancing together, he decided this was his calling and hopped over the fence to join in with an array of moves I could only assume he was doing to purposefully embarrass me and Riley.

But it was my sister who was happiest of all. As we stood for hour after hour watching everything unfold in an eruption of cheers and celebration, Riley might've just been the happiest person in the world.

'Isn't it *great*!' she exclaimed later as we sat on the corner of a quiet street waiting for Mum and Dad to get us some water from the shop. It was that lull in a summer's day, where the sun has started to fall in the sky, bathing everything it touches in a golden light. The air was a little cooler, entwined with a lingering thrill of excitement, the possibility that another adventure was just around the corner, that the day wasn't over just yet.

'I don't want it to end,' Riley added dreamily, a vague smile warming her face.

'I already want to do it all over again,' I agreed. Like I said, it was even better than the thrill of Thorpe Park.

'All these people here, they're like me in a way. This whole place feels like ... like home,' Riley breathed in wonder. I looked up at my sister, my heart fluttering as I'm sure hers was too. That's what London Pride was for my sister. It was home.

'Colour?' I asked, nudging her with my elbow.

You know those times when you can't find the right words to describe a feeling? It can be right there, sitting in the pit of your stomach or pumping through your body so you feel light and dizzy, but you just can't find the words in order to explain it to someone else? Well, Mum was always adamant that we should be able to talk about our feelings out loud.

'Keeping them locked up inside is good for nobody,' she'd say. So she would encourage us to think of a colour instead. It seemed a little silly at first, but then Mum showed us the swirls of paints on her palette and it actually made sense. Some colours are happier than others, or more vibrant and excited. Yellow, for example, or a light blue like the colour of a clear summer sky. Then there are the moody ones, like a dark purple that's almost black. If you ask me, that has to be the grumpiest colour of all.

Riley pondered the question, an even bigger smile stretching from ear to ear as she slung an arm around my shoulders. 'All of them,' she said. 'I feel every single colour of the rainbow.'

That was last summer, before everything else happened and when Dad was still with us. He was ill for a little while. I knew it was serious because Mum and Dad sat us down to tell us about it together. There were a lot of tears and promises that Dad was a fighter, and if anybody could get better again it was him. And then one day, he was just gone. I didn't understand how someone could be here one moment and then gone the next. In fact, I still don't. I guess we just always had hope that everything would be okay in the end, a little fire burning in each of us that warmed our coldest thoughts and gave us light in the dark.

Everything since then has been sort of grey, colourless in a way. I suppose that's why Pride is so special to me now – to all of us. It was our last day out together as a family, and the memory sits in my head, brimming with every colour of the rainbow. Colours we haven't been able to capture since.

And I guess that's where our story starts. There were a lot of things that changed after Dad passed away, but one of the biggest changes of all was hiding just around the corner.

CHAPTER 2

THE LEGENDARY FOOD FIGHT

ONE YEAR LATER

'DUCK!!!!!'

Lucas's warning leaped out of the din of King's Garden School canteen. I didn't know what I was ducking for, or from, but if your best friend yells 'DUCK', you don't sit there and wait to get hit in the face by a football or whatever's flying in your direction. My knees slammed into the floor as I disappeared under the table we'd been sitting at, just as a perfect square of Victoria sponge cake collided against the windowpane with a dull thud, exactly where my head had been. A roar of appreciation erupted from the other side of the hall.

'Food fight? Was that the big secret?' Lucas peeked

out from behind the table leg, his eyes, a dark brown like mine, darting around the canteen as a wicked smile lit up his face. We'd been best friends since the first day of Year Four, and I knew that smile meant trouble, something Lucas was only ever too happy to get into. 'Can you get detention on the last day of school?'

'Why do we have to waste a good dessert?' I sighed, reaching a hand out from under the table to find my own plate of Victoria sponge that I'd left behind. 'Couldn't they have served that other cake with the raisins in instead?' I took a quick bite, sighed once more, and grabbed the rest in my fist, grimacing slightly as it squelched into my palm. 'Dear God, please watch over this cake as it starts its journey towards Quentin's face.'

'Amen!' Lucas chorused.

Usually, I wouldn't recommend a Year Seven to start a fight with anybody in Year Eleven, but the rules were clearly out of the window today. And besides, Quentin had started it by throwing his Victoria sponge at us in the first place. Grinning, I jumped up and launched my cake in our attacker's direction, screaming a war cry that quickly turned into jubilation when it found its target. Unfortunately, my celebration didn't last long.

'Mum's going to kill me,' I gasped, ducking back under the table with a splodge of tomato ketchup dripping from my shirt collar. 'Is it in my hair? Please GOD tell me it isn't in my hair. I only washed it last night!'

A group of Year Elevens high-fived their success but hadn't noticed the creeping posse of Year Nines slinking round the corner with bowls of ketchup-drenched fries and mashed-up strawberries. The attack was quick, and mere seconds later, those who'd been celebrating looked as if they'd lost a fight against clowns. Poor Robbie Bratley, the Year Eleven prefect who'd been trying to calm the chaos down, now looked like a face-painting experiment that had been done in the dark.

And so the pandemonium began in earnest. There were shrieks from every direction as people realized what was happening. It was a tradition that even some of the teachers were in on – the Year Elevens, with freedom in sight as they prepared to move up into Sixth Form, were in charge of starting a prank that King's Garden wouldn't forget. It was like leaving their mark on the school, and everybody wanted to get involved.

'FIRE AWAY!!!!' Lucas yelled, rolling out from under the table with a fistful of chips, his curly hair bouncing as he went. He launched them hard and without direction. They splattered against the wall, five feet from the closest person.

'Nice shot,' I smirked, pinging leftover peas in the direction of a Year Eight who'd jumped the queue ahead of me to get into the canteen.

Food was flying everywhere, the day's menu sailing through the air and hitting anybody without cover. The lunch teachers tried to stop it, flailing their arms around in the air like that might stop an all-out war. Miss Anderson, who'd always been on the quieter side, had given up altogether and dived behind the kitchen counter for cover. I couldn't be certain, but when she peeped out from around the corner, I could've sworn I saw her mouthing 'good shot' as Polly Draper hit Big Bad Bob in the chest with a glob of jelly.

Lucas sprinted off to help ambush the football team, a seemingly personal vendetta considering he hadn't passed try-outs last year. I, on the other hand, was looking for a very specific target, but my sister was nowhere to be seen. Until ...

'Looking for someone?' I felt a warm sensation trickle down my back. I yelped but it was too late – Riley was standing with a now-empty bowl in her hand, her best friend Elmina giggling beside her. The custard was already soaking through my shirt.

'I told you not to wear something you might want to wear again,' Riley said, grinning. As a Year Eleven, she'd known what the prank was and had spent weeks refusing to tell me, something I took great offence to.

But Riley's jubilation was short-lived after she saw the bowl of jelly in my hand. 'You wouldn't *dare*,' she said, raising a forgotten plate of fries from a nearby table.

'Wouldn't I?' We raised our weapons at the same time, daring the other to fire first, but I didn't need any more encouragement. I drew the jelly back, took aim and . . .

'STOP WHAT YOU'RE DOING. RIGHT. NOW!' a stern voice bellowed, echoing around the canteen and stopping everybody in their tracks.

'What on EARTH is going on here?!' Mr Hudson was usually bright and chipper, but right at that very second, he was red with rage. I was trying my absolute hardest not to laugh, but I could feel it bubbling in my cheeks. Lucas was practically vibrating with barely contained giggles next to me which was making it ten times harder to control.

I think Mr Hudson must have been waiting for an

explanation or apology. Or maybe he was waiting for an army of mops to come twirling out of the cupboard and into our hands so the clean-up mission could begin. But what he actually got . . . well, I don't think it was what he was after.

It almost seemed to happen in slow motion. Mr Hudson didn't even see it coming. But the rest of us saw the jelly flying through the air as if it had wings. There was a united gasp as we realized it was going to make it. And then . . . *SPLAT*! It hit Mr Hudson square in the face, droplets of jelly exploding in every direction. I couldn't help but think that at least it was strawberry-flavoured.

Mr Hudson didn't even blink. He stood still as a statue, his face now pink from its jelly mask. An eerie silence fell over the canteen. For a moment, I thought time must've stopped still.

'Who . . . ?' Mr Hudson managed. His eyes roamed over us all, zeroing in on the most likely culprits.

'Ten pounds says it was Big Bad Bob,' Lucas whispered. I mulled this over. Bob was the best bet. He didn't have that name for no reason – he once threw Mr Waters's pencil case out of the window because Mr Waters said his drawing of a farm animal looked like a self-portrait.

But before I could offer my own bet, our deputy head teacher, Miss Moody, stepped forward. 'It was me,' she said steadily. My gasp was swallowed up by the collective hush that descended upon the canteen.

Mr Hudson blinked several times in shock, his lips parted before mashing together into a grim line. I'm sure I wasn't the only one holding my breath. It felt like the whole room was wide-eyed and watching. Mr Hudson nodded once to himself and I waited for the hammer to fall. Surely Miss Moody was about to get fired on the spot?

But instead, something quite different happened, something none of us saw coming. Our head teacher sighed, reached for a bowl of dessert, and threw its contents at Miss Moody. It landed with a splat right on her flowery blouse.

'I think that makes us even, Miss Moody,' Mr Hudson said.

And with that, the canteen descended into chaos once more.

The food fight would surely go down in history as the best King's Garden prank of all time. When the bell to signal the end of lunch had sounded, the whole room looked like it had been invaded by food-slinging aliens. Mr Hudson's declaration of war had really opened the floodgates.

Once everything had calmed down and the last ketchup-drenched fry had been thrown, our only punishment was cleaning up our mess while the teachers stood on the sidelines and barked orders. It wasn't exactly fair, considering they'd made a share of the mess themselves, but I think we could all agree it had been worth it.

Unfortunately, the rest of the school day stood between us and a summer of freedom. My final History lesson of the year was made even more miserable by the fact that I couldn't sit back in my chair now the custard puddle had dried into my shirt, making it all gross and sticky. But gossip about the summer ahead managed to keep my mind off things.

Rumours were already darting around about what we could expect at Tamera's birthday party at the end of July. Lucas and I kept mostly to ourselves, but Tamera was my desk buddy in English, which secured us both an invite. She'd be the last of us to turn twelve but would almost certainly do it more lavishly than anybody else. Early bets were on a bucking bronco or bouncy castle, but I personally thought my suggestion of a skydiving entrance should've been taken more seriously. All everybody knew for certain was that it was *definitely* something that couldn't be missed.

'I heard that Tamera's dad bought her an inflatable pool for the summer,' Lucas whispered dreamily from behind his rucksack, which he'd positioned so he wouldn't get caught napping while a documentary about the Tudors played in the background. 'We can have pool parties every weekend from now until September.'

'I heard she's also going to host a midsummer night's camping trip in her garden,' I whispered back, recalling the conversation in the girls' changing rooms before PE last week.

Whether all Tamera's claims were true was another matter, but her stories were much more fun to think about than a man with six wives. I could've sworn that the clock was ticking slower than usual towards 3.30 p.m. It wasn't just Lucas who was fighting the urge to nap – as the documentary droned on, half the class seemed to be using their desk as a pillow.

'We can go to a theme park,' I said, fighting a yawn

and urging the clock to hurry up as the final minutes trickled by.

'And the park next to the zoo!' Lucas was halfway out of his seat along with the rest of the class.

Three . . .

'Picnics!' I almost shouted with glee.

Two . . .

'Sleepovers!' Lucas added.

One . . .

'A whole summer of freedom!' I said, breathless with excitement.

There was a brief pause, a bloated silence filled with anticipation.

And then finally . . .

RING!!!!!

It felt as if everybody let out a breath at the same moment, jumping out of their seats, some even standing on top of them to celebrate. A tidal wave of noise started from somewhere on the other side of school, hurtling towards us. There were cheers and I felt them building up inside me until I could barely stop myself from bouncing up and down. Even the teachers looked relieved.

'Our summer awaits!' Lucas cheered. 'Six weeks of no

school, no teachers, no homework. Just us and the sun and more fun than we can imagine.'

A goofy grin spread over my face. I could hardly believe the school year was over. When we came back in September, we wouldn't be the new kids any more. But until then, we had a whole summer to look forward to, and not even a custard-stained shirt could dampen my excitement. Nothing was going to stand in our way.

CHAPTER 3

THIS IS NOT OUR HOME NOW

Like I said before, it's never usually good news when you walk through the front door to find your mum waiting at the kitchen table, so I stopped in my tracks when I saw her sitting there. All thoughts of which snack I was going to hustle up to my bedroom without her seeing trickled out of my mind, replaced by every terrible thing that could've possibly happened and now required a Kitchen Table Chat.

Mum's best friend, Rue, was also sat at the table: an old creaking thing that had been stuffed into the corner of our tiny kitchen so you couldn't fully open the back door. He was cradling a cup of coffee that I'd bet was his fourth of the day. You never saw Rue without a coffee in his hand. And you also never saw him without his husband, Travis, who I suddenly realized was leaning against the kitchen counter with a rather grave look on his face.

Riley, face buried in her phone and not looking where she was going as usual, crashed into my back. 'What're you doing?' she huffed. Then she saw Mum, Rue and Travis and quit her moaning. 'Are you getting a divorce?' Riley blurted accusingly in Travis and Rue's direction, panic stretching its mask across her face.

Rue, always the more dramatic of the two, spat out his coffee. He was tall and slim, with gleaming brown skin that seemed to reflect the sun itself. Whenever he spoke, it was like he'd swallowed a microphone. Travis folded his lips together, trying to keep the laugh in his cheeks. He was shorter and wider and spoke in a slow, deep voice. Quiet and calm, he was the perfect counterbalance to Rue.

Mum laughed too, but it was stiff and without real humour. I stayed rooted to the spot, suspicious and afraid that if I stepped one foot into the kitchen, the whole floor might give way and we'd all go crashing through it. Maybe the bad news wouldn't be able to reach us if we stayed out in the hallway.

'You mean get rid of this big oaf? Let me know if you've

come up with a plan for that one – all of mine have failed so far.' Rue winked in Travis's direction.

'No divorce,' Travis confirmed. The ghost of a laugh was already gone from his face as he glanced over at Mum. She bowed her head and cleared her throat.

'Can you come and sit down for a second? I need to talk to you both,' she said quietly.

Another thing that's never good news . . . If someone says, 'Can we talk?' you have to immediately start thinking the worst has happened and work backwards from there. Don't blame me – I don't make the rules. It's just how it is.

It had to be something serious if Mum had brought Rue and Travis over for backup. It wasn't unusual to see them here, especially after the year we'd had. They kept Mum company and brought a bubble of happiness to the house, the kind we'd been missing. But this clearly wasn't good news, so I started running through a list of potential disasters in my head, still not moving from my spot in the doorway. Riley wasn't even trying to push past me, so I was sure she was doing the same.

'Did someone die?' I asked cautiously, not sure if I wanted to know the answer. Mum flinched and I felt Riley tense up behind me. I probably could've worded that a bit better, but I wanted to be prepared this time.

'Can you both just come in here and sit down?' Mum sighed. 'I'll explain everything then.'

'So someone *is* dead,' I murmured to myself. I was trying to breathe normally but it was as if I'd forgotten how. My heart felt like it was beating in the back of my throat.

'Bea.' Mum didn't use her stern voice very often, so I shrugged and tentatively stepped into the kitchen, still half-expecting to fall through the floor. Thoughts of impending doom pecked at the inside of my head. I tried to ignore them as I picked my usual seat and slung my bag over the back of the chair, waiting for the bad news to come. And oh boy, did it.

'We're moving to Gran's for the summer,' Mum said simply, ripping the plaster off. I don't want you to think I was being dramatic or anything, but it felt like the breath in my lungs all escaped at once.

'WHAT?!' Riley and I cried in unison.

'I told you they'd take it badly,' Rue murmured, raising his eyebrows in Travis's direction. Mum gave him a pointed glance before taking a deep breath and facing us again. She looked more uncomfortable than I'd ever seen her before.

'Look, I'm going to be honest with you, and I need you both to be grown-ups, okay?' I sat up a little straighter, happy to be in on an adult's conversation for once. Riley didn't quite feel the same, judging by her reaction – her face had scrunched itself together like she'd just smelled something rotten.

Mum sighed, long and deep. 'Things are tough right now. Since your dad ...' She faltered, but only briefly, clearing her throat once more. 'Since your dad died, we've been struggling. With money, I mean. I thought I could keep on top of it but ... well, the rent's long overdue and at the rate we're going, we won't have any gas or electric next month. I've tried picking up extra shifts, but it'd take a whole lot more than that to keep us afloat.'

Mum had always been an artist, but it never paid much. Dad said she should do what she loved and to hell with money so long as we had each other. But when he died, she'd had no choice but to find something else, and she started working shifts at a corner shop down the street. Painting had taken a back seat since then.

Mum was tearing up, great pools forming in her eyes

and threatening to burst at any moment. It made me want to reach across the table and throw my arms around her, but I felt trapped in my seat, the weight of my own thoughts pinning me down. This was our home. It had been since before I could even remember. It was the only place we'd known and, with Dad gone, it felt as though a piece of him was still here with us, like he was just around the corner ready to burst through the front door and fall on to the sofa with a newspaper under his arm. I used to tell myself that would happen in the beginning, that he was just at the shop getting milk and bread, or that he was working a really long shift at the hospital. But, of course, he never walked through the door. I toughed it out on the surface, mostly because I didn't want to give anybody another reason to worry, another reason to be sad. But, between you and me, it felt like a hole had opened up inside me, a void that stretched bigger and bigger, impossible to fill.

'I'm sorry,' Mum was saying, dragging me out of my thoughts and into the room once more. 'I've tried everything I can think of but it's not working. Mr Thorpe has given us two weeks' notice and there's nothing I can do about it. We don't have enough time to find somewhere else, but if he wants us to go then we have no choice. Gran's is the only option we have left.'

I'd always hated Mr Thorpe. Sure, he technically owned the bricks and concrete and everything else, but I didn't care about that – this was *our* house, and I couldn't believe he could just take it away from us like that. Mum hiccoughed and bowed her head, her shoulders shaking. Rue reached across the table and took her hand in his, muttering something under his breath about landlords.

'So, that's it then?'

A cold shiver ran over my body. I could tell by Riley's voice – the stilted, punchy words – that she wasn't happy. Far from it. She'd taken the news about Dad worse than anybody. When it happened, it was like a light inside her just suddenly switched off, dragging her deeper into darkness and leaving the rest of us to wonder where she'd gone. Sometimes a glimmer of the old Riley would appear, when she would laugh at old reruns of shows we loved, or when she was singing in the shower. But then she'd catch herself and disappear again.

'I've tried everything, Ry. I really have. We need the chance to reset, to get back on our feet, save some money and start afresh. It'll only be for a couple of months.

We'll be back in London before the summer's over. I promise.'

'Back in London, but not back here, you mean?' Riley's face was clouding over with the white-hot rage that'd been constantly simmering just out of sight since Dad had gone.

Mum bit her lip, wiping her eyes with the back of her sleeve. Rue and Travis looked like they wanted the ground to open up and swallow them whole. 'We'd have you at ours, but we barely have enough room for ourselves,' Travis said apologetically.

'We'll find somewhere else,' Mum tried.

'I'm not going,' Riley said bluntly, folding her arms. 'I'm not moving to Gran's. I'm not leaving London, I'm not leaving my friends, and I'm not leaving our home.'

'We don't have a choice. Mr Thorpe has a new family ready to move in. It's already done.' Riley went to open her mouth to say God knows what, but Mum beat her to the punch. 'Riley, *please*. I don't want to leave our home any more than you do, but when I say we don't have a choice, I mean it. Don't take this out on me. I've done everything I can to keep this family afloat and I'd appreciate it if you'd sho—'

Riley snorted and I knew all hell was about to break

loose. I glanced at Rue for help, but he just grimaced and pretended to take a sip from the coffee cup I knew was empty.

'Well, I'm staying here. You can't *make* me do anything. I'm nearly an adult,' Riley shot back.

'You're sixteen, and for another few months by my calendar. You're a *child* and you'll do as I say.' Mum's tears were replaced with a fire that matched Riley's. 'This conversation is over. We're moving to St Regent's Vale for the summer, and that's final.'

Riley fixed Mum with a glare that could've shattered glass or melted solid concrete, one that made me shrink back into my chair because it reminded me how much of my sister we'd lost. She'd always been the quiet one. Now, she was mad at the world, and we all knew why. Mum met Riley's glare with one of her own. Riley had inherited it from her in the first place, so she was never going to win that battle. I sank lower in my seat, praying it'd all be over soon.

'It won't be so bad,' Travis tried gently. Rue shot him a panicked look, but Travis just shrugged. 'A summer out in the country, all that fresh air and space – sounds like a holiday to me!'

'*You* go then,' Riley huffed.

I wanted to say something, to try and make things better, just like I'd been doing for the past year. When everything fell apart, all I'd wanted to do was piece it back together again. But now nothing would come. A thousand thoughts swirled around my head, questions popping out and ducking behind each other before I could grab them and make sense of it all.

Riley sniffed and I felt the fight leave her, like it'd just packed its bags, climbed out of her body and walked straight out of the front door. Her shoulders sagged and she bowed her head. Mum didn't have any words of comfort that would've solved the problem. Neither did Rue or Travis.

Riley suddenly shot out of her chair, her cheeks wet from tears that she wasn't even trying to hide any more. Without a backward glance, she bolted from the kitchen and up the stairs, slamming her bedroom door for good measure. A shadow of exhaustion passed over Mum's face as she dropped it into her hands.

'Bea? Can you do me a favour please?'

I nodded, even if I didn't know what it was yet. I wasn't about to rock the boat any further, even if the boat had already sunk. 'Wait ten minutes and then go and check on your sister.'

'Sure,' I mumbled, jumping off the chair and grabbing my bag, my head spinning from everything running around inside it.

'Well, that's the tough bit out of the way,' I heard Rue murmur. I peeked around the banister in time to see Mum fall into his open arms. Travis came up behind them and wrapped himself around them both, giving them a tight squeeze.

'I miss you both already,' mumbled Mum.

'Oh please,' Rue said with a wave of his hand. 'Like you'll get rid of us that easily! We're coming to visit. You just try and stop us.'

Thoughts of Rue and Travis arriving in St Regent's Vale and brightening the whole place up made me smile for a second. Then I remembered my sister, how I'd have to break the news to Lucas, how my summer plans had just erupted before I'd even had a chance to enjoy one of them. With a deep sigh, I started the long climb up the stairs and into the dark, knowing that things were probably going to get a whole lot worse from here.

CHAPTER 4

BLACK IS THE DARKEST COLOUR

My parents used to say that my sister and I were like winter and summer, my sister all soft sunlight and peaceful days, me the complete opposite. According to Mum, Riley was as quiet as a mouse the moment she was born and barely cried at all. As for me? Well, I came into the world like a crash of thunder and made enough noise for the both of us.

Riley used to be as gentle as a breath of wind. She could sit still for ages, face in her phone or reading her books or just *thinking* about things. I've never been very good at sitting still — I fidget and think about moving until eventually I have to get up and do something — but Riley could daydream for hours, not looking at anything in particular and just living inside her own head. She'd been doing that more and more lately. It was like a superpower that only teenagers are allowed. I sometimes wonder if I'll be the same when I turn thirteen.

But since Dad had died, there'd been a switch. Now I was summer, trying to soothe everything with my light, to make everything bright and happy again. And Riley was winter, like a coldness had settled inside her.

As if we couldn't be more opposite, we don't really look the same either. Riley's almost as tall as Mum already, and if they sat side by side, you'd be able to see one in the other. They share the same dark skin, smooth as a blank piece of paper, and the same dark brown eyes that can shut you up with one firm look. They have the same straight nose, which crinkles on either side when they smile. Riley's had braids since her fourteenth birthday, which she twists into various knots to keep them out of her face when she's trying to concentrate. Mum dealt with that problem by cutting most of her own hair off. She said it just got in the way when she was trying to paint and now it's one less thing to worry about.

Me? I'm more of an even mix of Mum and Dad, like a swirl of ingredients that both of them added to the bowl. I'm Black – of course, because both of them are too – and, to be honest, kind of small. I'm waiting on my next growth spurt, which I'm sure has to be due any day now. I have Mum's eyes and cheeks, Dad's nose and mouth, and apparently my great-grandad's attitude, but I'm not sure if that's a good thing. Unlike Riley and Mum, I let my hair grow out into an afro, the curls flowing out around my head. I don't know how long it'll grow yet, but I won't stop until I'm like a Black Rapunzel.

There wasn't an answer when I knocked on Riley's door (seven minutes earlier than Mum had told me to) so I gently pushed it open and peeked my head inside. She was curled up on her bed, one of her giant hoodies that's at least two sizes too big wrapped around her. She loves to get lost inside its folds when she's in a bad mood, so this wasn't exactly looking great.

'Not now, Bea,' Riley muttered, not bothering to roll over and face the door because she already knew it'd be me.

I ignored her request and padded into the room, long shadows from the houses behind ours swamping it in gloom. I flicked the lamp on and hopped on to the bed. Riley wrapped the hoodie around herself tighter and ignored me.

'Colour?' I said, settling into the open arms of the enormous teddy Riley had owned since she was a baby. He was called Barry, which doesn't seem like a bear's name to me but hey, it wasn't my choice.

'Black,' Riley replied bluntly. Black seemed ... well, a little dramatic, but it explained Riley's mood perfectly.

'It's really that bad, huh ... ?' I was thinking out loud to myself, still on the edge of sulking about a whole summer of plans that now lay in ruins. I knew this was about more than just my summer holidays, but that didn't mean I was happy about it either.

Riley sat up straight and shot me a glare, taking my words as a personal insult. She'd been doing that a lot lately. 'Yes, it's *that* bad,' she said, sweeping a loose braid out of her face so she could glare at me some more. 'Did you not hear Mum? We're leaving this place for ever and we're never coming back. This is our house and now it's just ...' She threw her hands up in the air and slumped back down on to the pillow, staring at the ceiling. 'There's nothing even *in* St Regent's Vale anyway, except a bunch of fields and mud. I'm not going.'

Riley had a point – seeing Gran was great, but St Regent's Vale was hardly a hub of excitement. We hadn't been there in a long time, what with it being so far away. And since Dad got sick, Mum's visits had stalled too. Usually, she'd go and stay for a few nights every couple of months. She'd ask us if we wanted to go with her, but we always managed to come up with some excuse to stay home. We'd only *had* to go if Dad was working. To put it simply, St Regent's Vale was a small pocket tucked away in the countryside where boredom itself could end up bored.

Moving to the small village that Mum grew up in might not have sounded like the end of the world – it might've sounded like an adventure actually, if you looked at it with the right perspective – but it wasn't home. Sure, we'd only be there for a summer, but that didn't change the fact that when we came back to London, we wouldn't be coming back here. The bigger picture was slowly coming into focus, the disruption of my summer plans moving out of the way to reveal what else could change. It made me feel nervous and a little sick.

'And we'll miss it,' Riley murmured, more to herself.

'Miss what?' I frowned, unsure whether she was still talking about the house or Dad.

'Pride,' Riley said quietly.

She rolled over to face me as memories from last year

flooded my mind. It seemed too dramatic to say it was the last time we'd been happy. Of course, we'd found snippets of happiness since then, but they were nothing more than pockets of light and hope in the darkness.

Without another word, Riley sat up and fell to her knees next to the bed, rooting around underneath it. She pulled out a box that had been decorated with stickers and sketches and glitter. From the way she held it, all gentle and delicate, I knew it must be important. I sat up straight, ready to be let in on a secret.

Riley placed the box between us on the bed and lifted the lid. Inside were a bunch of pictures and slips of paper, scrunched-up tickets and flyers with rainbows swirling over the pages. It was our day, just as I remembered it – colourful and exciting, wondrous and magical. A warm feeling tingled over my skin, as if lifting the lid off the box had let it escape.

Riley grabbed a stack of the pictures and spread them out in front of us. They were Polaroid snapshots, with captions scribbled in coloured ink on the white space underneath the photo. There were Riley and Mum hugging each other tightly and grinning into the camera. Another was of me and Riley surrounded by people wearing impossibly high heels and even taller wigs. Both of us were gazing in wonder as one of the drag queens threw their head back in laughter at something I couldn't remember. The next snap was Mum and Dad, arm in arm, looking at each other as if they were the only two people in the world. I brought the picture up to my face, like I could somehow be closer to that day if I tried hard enough. It took all my effort to drag my eyes away and focus on something else.

There were pictures of the crowds, more people and colour than I remembered; dancers and singers and street performers cloaked in rainbows and feathers and sparkle; the parade itself, which seemed to stretch up the street for miles, majestic floats frozen in time like mythical creatures. There were snaps of places I recognized, the landmarks of London I knew all too well. But they didn't look like they did when you saw them on a regular day. Trafalgar Square looked like it was celebrating a summer Christmas, with streamers and bunting strung between the statues. In another snapshot, the lights of Piccadilly Circus flashed proudly over the parade below, a rainbow flag plastered over its huge screens.

And then the final two pictures. The first was Riley,

caught mid-laugh in a storm of confetti. It was as if pure happiness was showering over her and, even though she'd tried to cover her face as she laughed, you couldn't miss the joy. That was my sister before, when she was the happiest girl in the world. I missed seeing her like that.

The last picture had been taken at the end of the day, with the sun dipping low in the sky. Riley and me stood between Mum and Dad, our grins wide. I could hear Dad saying, 'On three, say "we're proud of you, Riley",' and we'd all chorused it together. Underneath the picture was a small heart and, in Riley's looping scrawl, the word: 'FAMILY!'

I snuck a glance at my sister, who looked exactly how I felt with the pictures laid out between us. But the golden filter started to fade as she floated back down to Earth, her smile vanishing.

'I was looking forward to feeling like this again,' she said, her hand drifting over the photo of herself laughing and coming to rest on one of her between Mum and Dad, wrapped in a hug. Her eyes started to shimmer as she scooped it up.

'I'm scared that we'll lose him, Bea. Like, what if we forget how his voice sounds, or the pictures we have of him in our heads start to blur and fade? It's like there's a part of him here because it's our home, and there's a part of him there too, at Pride. I know it. He'd want us to go again, even if he can't be there with us.'

Tears of my own were bubbling up inside me and threatening to spill over the walls I'd built to keep them at bay. Riley wouldn't look at me. She wasn't even looking at anything in the room. She was staring off at something that only she could see.

'We can't miss Pride and we can't leave our home.' Her voice broke as she lay back down, holding the picture close to her chest. 'We can't leave him behind.'

I didn't know what to say to that, but apparently I didn't need to say anything. Riley shrugged, rolling away to face the wall. 'It's okay, Bea. I just wanna be on my own.'

I knew when to leave my sister alone with her thoughts, so I slipped out of the room quietly and nearly yelped the house down when I bumped into Mum and Rue standing outside the door, lurking in the shadows like two teenagers who'd been caught doing something wrong. Mum quickly put a finger to her lips in panic, clearly embarrassed that they'd been caught.

'What did she say?' Mum whispered.

'Is she all right?' Rue added.

'If you're going to talk about me, can you at least do it somewhere where I *can't* hear?' Riley's voice huffed from behind her bedroom door. Mum and Rue grimaced while Travis sighed from the bottom of the stairs. Then Mum pulled me into a hug and disappeared back down to the kitchen, no doubt to do more talking about Riley and me and St Regent's Vale.

Meanwhile, I was left to my own thoughts, memories of Pride flitting through my head like a montage, one dashing past to be replaced with another. Seeing those pictures had reminded me of a time that almost didn't feel real any more – a time when we were a whole family, together like any other. I would've given anything to go back and live that day one last time. Instead, like Riley, I feared that with each day, the memory would fade away. And that was the thing I was most scared of – what if I started to forget? What if traces of that memory, all the little details that made it perfect, slipped away like a dream in the morning, like water in my hands? What if?

CHAPTER 5

SULKING IS FOR TODDLERS AND SOON-TO-BE-TEENAGERS WHO HAVE TO LEAVE THEIR FRIENDS FOR THE SUMMER

With less than a week to go before our 'adventure' to St Regent's Vale – that's what Mum was trying to call it anyway – the days that followed were miserable at best. It was like the carpet in our house was actually made of eggshells. The slightest misstep could send any one of us spiralling into a void of emotions, none of them good. The mood in our house was like a bad case of the flu lingering in every nook and cranny, and as the big moving day drew closer, things only seemed to be getting worse.

As I'd predicted, Riley was taking it the worst of us all. I mean, I wasn't exactly jumping for joy at the prospect of moving house, much less packing for St Regent's Vale of all places, but Riley was acting like the whole thing was a personal offence. Since the whole sit-down thing, she'd taken up residence in her room and was refusing to leave it other than for emergencies. Those emergencies were limited to:

1. Hoarding snacks when she thought nobody else was in the kitchen.
2. Brushing her teeth because even though she was thoroughly miserable, there's never really an excuse to not at least do that.
3. Leaving the house altogether on rare occasions to see Elmina, but only when the coast was clear and Mum couldn't attempt to corner her for another talk.

Other than that, Riley was more than happy to stay barricaded in her own bedroom. In fact, it almost seemed like she was choosing to believe that the rest of us didn't exist. She was ignoring Mum at all costs as if it were her fault entirely that we were moving. She was barely even talking to me, and I hadn't done anything wrong!

I don't know if I'm getting this across to you well enough, but just so we're all on the same page – our entire house was completely, utterly *miserable* and I was beginning to hate every second inside it. So I escaped it at every opportunity, finding solace with Lucas in our secret den.

Our hideout was one that had been passed down through generations. My dad had grown up nearby and used to while away the summer days with his own friends in the small pocket of space that nobody even thought about any more. It wasn't much – just a square of dirt that was meant to be an allotment tucked behind a newsagent's, a charity shop and a nail salon, set back from the bustling city road. There were a couple of abandoned sheds that had definitely seen better days, as well as a crumbling garage that hadn't been used since before even Dad's time. If you ducked under its buckled metal door, there were remnants of the kids who'd used it as their den over the years: crumpled magazines and empty packets of crisps littered the floor. The dust was everywhere, forming a thick layer around parts of the garage that basically hadn't been touched since the Middle Ages. There was a sofa too, squashed and sunken in on itself from decades of butts and trainers. It wasn't much, but it was ours. And it was where I'd planned to break the news to Lucas.

He took it as well as I'd expected, which is to say ... terribly. I'd thought of a million different ways to say it, but whichever way I rehearsed it, the story was still the same – I was leaving for the summer, and that was that. Lucas, ever dramatic, sank to the floor with his hand pressed to his forehead like an old Hollywood actress, crying out to the clouds above that all was ruined. Like I said, dramatic.

'When will you be back?' he grumbled once he'd got himself together and back to his feet. He kicked a patch of weeds that'd broken through the concrete and began pacing in a sulk.

'End of summer,' I mumbled.

'That's the *whoooooole* summer holidays!' Lucas moaned.

'Thanks for reminding me,' I said darkly, trying to push thoughts of everything Lucas would do without me while I was at Gran's house out of my head. The sleepovers were the main source of my jealousy – the best secrets and school gossip always got spilled at those. But it was the thought of Tamera's birthday party that was really kicking me in the gut. I'd have given up chocolate digestives for a year to be there. Now, when we returned to school in September, I'd be the only one who couldn't be included in the conversations about how great it was. As someone who hates to be left out of just about anything, I was seething about this part in particular.

'You can't be gone for the *whole* summer. What am *I* meant to do if you're not here?' With the way he was moaning, anybody would've thought it was Lucas going to spend the holidays in the middle of nowhere.

'Enjoy the summer without me, I guess,' I muttered sourly.

'You can stay at mine!' Lucas chirped, stopping in the middle of the garage like he'd just come up with a genius idea. Then another thought crossed his mind and he faltered. 'I'm sure my mum won't mind . . .' He sounded uncertain of that fact.

Lucas continued narrating his every thought about how this was grossly unfair and a violation of our right to have an unforgettable summer. Between his woe-be-me monologue, Riley's darkening moods and the prospect of leaving our house for ever, my own feelings of annoyance were building. If I had it my way, I'd be staying put with everything just as it was.

'Riley's mad about the whole thing,' I said once Lucas had got the majority of his moaning out of his system. 'She's furious actually.'

'Well, it's obvious why, isn't it?' Lucas said, grinning like he was in on a well-kept secret. 'She'll have to leave her girlfriend behind.'

I frowned. 'She doesn't have a girlfriend,' I said, although less sure now in the face of Lucas's smirk. If my sister had a girlfriend, I'd be the first to know about it . . . right? Once upon a time, there wouldn't have been a single thing my sister would've kept from me. But that was before everything had happened, and before this ever-widening void came between us.

'That's not what *I* saw,' Lucas carried on, now looking more smug than ever. He pretended to zip his lips.

'Spit it out then – what *did* you see?' I said, not entirely sure I actually wanted to be led down this path. Lucas cleared his throat, enjoying the spotlight a little too much, I thought. He looked like he would've grabbed a microphone and a stage if he could.

'Well,' he started, his voice grand with dramatic

excitement. I rolled my eyes and sighed. 'I was coming back from the park and I saw Riley sitting on a bench with *Taylor*—'

'The girl who wore red lipstick on the last day of school and got sent home?' I butted in. It had been quite the mini-scandal.

'Yeah! That one!' Lucas clapped his hands together like he'd cracked the case. I waited for the rest but . . . nothing.

'Okaaaaaaay,' I said impatiently, trying not to huff and puff because Mum hates it when I do that. She thinks it's rude, but Lucas was testing my good manners. 'And then what happened?'

Lucas shifted under my watch, squirming and clasping his hands together. 'Well, I didn't exactly *see* anything else.' He deflated a little, and he was mumbling now too – never a good sign.

'You saw Riley and Taylor sitting on a bench together? And that's it?' I scoffed, suddenly leaping away from him in mock horror. 'Don't stand too close! People might think we're girlfriend and boyfriend!' Lucas scowled and kicked an empty can in my direction.

'So, you're really not gonna be here for the whole summer?' he asked quietly when I'd got my giggles back under control. 'It's not going to be the same without you here.'

I tried not to pout because I'm twelve years old and that kind of sulking is for toddlers. But I couldn't help it. Whichever way I looked at the situation, it sucked. It really, really sucked.

CHAPTER 6

THE ART OF PACKING

If being in a bad mood was an Olympic sport, Riley would have won a platinum medal. I know that kind of medal doesn't really exist, but gold wouldn't have been nearly good enough for the mood Riley was in. It was quite possibly the worst mood on record.

Mum wasn't faring much better herself, which came as a surprise to me considering she was the rock of the family, the glue that kept us all together. If Mum was fine, then we knew everything would turn out okay in the end. But I'd caught Mum crying and weeping behind various closed doors in the house and, for once, I was starting to think that maybe things wouldn't be okay after all.

As for me? Well, with Mum temporarily out of action

when it came to making us all feel better, and Riley in a mood so foul that it threatened to engulf everything it came into contact with, it was up to me to try and be as upbeat as possible, even if everything seemed ... well, pretty terrible.

But even I couldn't keep my spirits up when packing began in earnest, and my mood was looking a little more like Riley's by the time the day of the Big Move was upon us. If you ask me, the art of packing is pretty simple.

STEP ONE: Don't.

STEP TWO: Repeat step one.

'This doesn't look like packing to me,' Mum said from nowhere, making me jump so high that I nearly fell off the bed.

'I was just packing, I swear.' Mum scanned my bedroom floor and raised a single eyebrow in my direction at the sight of it. 'Well, I was about to anyway, I promise.' Mum breathed a laugh and came to sit on my bed, picking up an old book, its cover bound in cracked leather.

'I haven't seen this in a long time,' Mum said, flipping through the first few pages with a smile spreading across her face like early morning sunlight.

It was my baby book, the one Mum and Dad had made

for me when I was born. Riley had one too somewhere. It marked all the big occasions and markers I couldn't remember, like how much I weighed when I came into the world, the day I took my first steps, how tall I was on my first day of nursery. There were some pictures too, of toddler birthday parties and awful dungarees that I was only too happy were no longer in my possession. I scrunched up my nose at some of the outfit choices but none of the pictures were as embarrassing as the one where I was wearing socks on my ears like pigtails. Mum laughed, pulling me into a one-armed hug.

As she flicked the pages once more, my breath caught in my throat and Mum tensed up beside me. There was a photo of us all together. I was five or six, Riley a few years older than that and standing slightly turned away from the camera as if getting her picture taken was the most mortifying chore she could've been asked to do. I stood at the front, hands on my hips like I was sizing up the person taking the picture and deciding whether I could trust them or not. Mum, who actually had hair then because it was that long ago, had a grin so wide that it could've been brighter than all the stars in the galaxy combined. Dad had his half-smile stuck in place like he always did when a camera was pointed in his direction, his hand resting on my shoulder as if worried I might run at the photographer and kick them in the shins.

I rested my head on Mum as I took in the scene, my eyes and cheeks tingling. I heard Mum sniff and hugged her tighter.

'I miss him,' I said, my voice all small and wobbly.

Mum sighed, rubbing circles into my arm. 'We all do.'

A creak at the bedroom door made us both jump and Riley almost looked shocked that she'd been caught. I bit my lip, hoping we weren't in for another fight.

'You want to come in?' Mum asked, patting the spot next to her on the bed. Riley looked at it and then over at us, her eyes sizing everything up like there could be a trap just waiting out of sight.

'Ry ...' Mum tried, but that did it. Like a mouse that had been caught in the dead of night, Riley turned on her heel and flew back into her bedroom, leaving the doorway empty once more. Mum let out a long breath and started to get up, closing the book and laying it safely back on the bed. When I saw her face, it was tear-stained and exhausted.

'You okay, Mum?' I asked. She waved me off with a flick of her hand and a shake of her head.

'I'll be fine once you get over here and give me another hug.' I bounded over and wrapped my arms around her. 'You okay, Bumble?' That was my nickname since I was little, when Riley couldn't say my name without buzzing around the room impersonating a bee. Mum pulled away after a second and held me at arm's length to get a better look at me. You couldn't lie when she did that, but I gave it my best go.

'Mmhmm. Fine, just sleepy.' My real feelings were behind those walls, trying to peek their heads out. But I clamped them back down. If I told myself I was okay, then soon enough I would be. I refused to be mad at everything like Riley.

Mum narrowed her eyes but decided not to call me out as Pinocchio. 'We're out of here early in the morning so all of this needs to be packed and ready for storage before bedtime.'

'Ughhhhhhh,' I moaned, eyeing up everything that was still waiting to be put in boxes.

'No whining or complaining – up and at 'em. This room has to be sparkling by the time we leave, so get to it. And don't be afraid of a bit of polish either. That bottle don't bite, you know.' Mum ran a finger along my dresser, glancing over at me with pursed lips before retreating back downstairs.

I picked up the baby book and flipped it open to one of the last pages. There was a picture of me sitting on Dad's shoulders, beaming at the camera with every tooth in my head. I wished I was on his shoulders again, taller than everybody else and laughing wildly together like we always did. If he were here now, he'd let us know that everything would be okay, I was sure of it. And holding on to that little nugget of hope, I closed the baby book and placed it safely in my backpack.

CHAPTER 7

GOODBYE FOR NOW

I woke up the next morning and, for a second, I forgot about everything. It was something I'd grown used to over the past year, and a brief moment I'd grown to savour too. In the haze of morning, when sleep and dreams were still clinging to me, I'd forget – forget that Dad wasn't here, that our family now had this aching space where he should've been. But then, as it always did, sleep would slip away, and I'd remember. It was like being hit by an unyielding wave, one that pulled me under time and time again as reality came flooding back.

We were leaving our home today, and we wouldn't be coming back. This would be the last time I'd ever get to call this place home. I stood in the doorway of my bedroom, now bare and empty, the sky-blue paint of the walls (a colour I'd been allowed to pick) the only thing left that marked it out as mine. The removal men had arrived even earlier than Mum had said, knocking us out of bed with more noise than was acceptable for that time of the morning and carting all our furniture out into the back of a big van. Unless I wanted to be packed off to a storage unit, I had no choice but to get out of bed and let them take it from me, although I won't lie, for a brief moment I did think about hiding under the mattress and staying in London that way.

Mum was running around like a headless chicken, clucking to herself as she made the final checks around the house. Riley had emerged from her bedroom, her face mostly hidden by the hood of her sweater that she'd drawn up around her head. It wasn't a good sign, but at least she hadn't decided to handcuff herself to the banisters in protest. The fact she was leaving the house on her own two feet and not being dragged out by Mum was a small victory I was willing to savour.

'Can you believe that's just like … our life?' I mused as I joined my sister at the front door, staring out at our car which was nearly overflowing with the belongings we were taking to Gran's with us.

'Our whole life in one vehicle,' Riley muttered, folding her arms and glaring at the car like it had just called her a mean name. 'I've never seen anything so sad in my life.' Shaking her head, Riley stormed towards the passenger seat and threw herself inside.

'Ready, Bumble?' Mum said, scooting up behind me and double-checking the contents of her bag.

'I guess,' I mumbled. I took a deep breath, willing my feet to step over the doorstep and on to the pavement. It was such a small thing, it should've been easy enough. But I couldn't do it. I knew that as soon as I took that step, there was no going back.

Mum sensed something was wrong and rested her hand on my shoulder. 'Let's do it together, shall we?' She grabbed my hand and counted to three. With another big breath, we stepped outside into the early morning sunlight.

Before Mum locked the door behind us, I took one last peek into our house. At the end of the short corridor was the kitchen door, where there were still colourful lines on the frame that Dad had made to mark our height as we grew up. When I saw it, a lump formed in my throat. Then Mum closed the door and it was gone.

Mum didn't turn around immediately, though. Like me, she stayed facing the door for a moment, resting her hand against the pale wood. Then, with a watery smile, she nodded to herself and got into the car, clearing her throat of things I'm sure she wanted to say but didn't know how to.

How do you even say goodbye to the house you've known all your life? I wanted to do something, anything, to mark the occasion, to say goodbye properly. But no grand ideas came to me. The only thought that crept into my brain was of Dad, and I had a feeling I wasn't the only one who was thinking of him now. Everything I'd ever known of my dad, all the things we'd done together, had happened in that house – sliding down the stairs in our duvets, burning my first attempt at pancakes, watching wrestling TV shows that I'd only been interested in for two weeks before I moved on to something else. I just hoped that those memories were coming with us, and that Dad was too.

'Are we there yet?' I whined, trying not to sulk in the back.

I'm not one to be dramatic – okay, maybe I am a little bit – but it felt like we'd been driving for a million years. I'm sure the drive never usually felt this long. We'd left the city behind us a long time ago and now there was nothing but green for as far as the eye could see. It's not like I was expecting the trees to be blue or anything, but something *other* than green would've been a welcome sight.

'We're five minutes closer than the last time you asked,' Mum said, just as sulky and irritated.

The endless traffic of London had given way to the wide roads of the motorway until we'd taken an exit which led into winding countryside lanes, the open fields divided from the road by hedgerows that zipped by my window in a blur. We'd taken a wrong turn an hour back and nobody had realized until we started to see signs for a city that was nowhere near where we needed to be. Mum was still grumpy about that even though, as the driver of the car, it was technically her fault. Out of sheer boredom, I'd reminded her of that information. Let's just say it didn't exactly go down very well.

'Finally,' I muttered as a weather-worn plaque promised

that St Regent's Vale was only three miles away. My bum was starting to go numb from all the sitting.

Mum slowed the car down as we pulled into the village, which seemed like the right thing to do considering St Regent's Vale appeared to be asleep. It was like somebody had pulled a blanket over the village square and said goodnight.

'It's so quiet,' I said suspiciously. All this silence couldn't possibly mean good news if you asked me. Back in London, the closest thing you got to peace was a wailing car alarm harmonizing with the honk of a taxi in the middle of the night.

'Isn't it lovely?' Mum murmured, as if she were afraid of waking somebody up.

'It's making me itch,' Riley muttered, wrapping her arms around herself.

Gran's cottage was tucked away behind a large tree and framed with ivy that clung to the brick and haloed the windows. At first sight, you might've been fooled into thinking it was a bungalow, but when you stepped under the canopy of the oak, you could see smaller windows peeking out of the roof, baskets of flowers hanging from their ledges. There was a perfectly manicured front garden – something our house (which opened up on to the concrete pavement) couldn't even dream of – with three wheelie bins lined up perfectly next to the driveway. The one in the middle had been painted with an array of colourful flowers, which just added to the picture. Out back, the garden stretched down to a line of shrubs, which divided it from the wild, wide-open fields beyond. It was paradise, if you were into that sort of thing. I wasn't sure about it yet.

Gran stood on the front step as we clambered out of the car, like she'd been waiting there for days. A broad grin was trying its best to take over her whole face as she took us all in, her arms spread wide in welcome.

'Hi, Gran,' I said, skipping over the lawn and wrapping myself up in one of her hugs. Riley swooped in behind me and added herself into the equation. She might've been in a bad mood, but that was nothing to do with Gran.

Gran was a small old lady who walked with a slight hunch and plenty of complaints as she hobbled from one place to another. I'd only ever known her with grey hair, and it was set into short, tight curls. She smelled the same as she always did – bright and flowery – and I breathed it in as she hugged us back.

'You too, Cammie. Get in here,' Gran beckoned. Mum

fell into the group hug without question. The four of us held on to each other, with me, as the smallest of us all, cocooned in the middle.

'It's about time I had you all out here with me. I was beginning to think I'd never get you out of that rotten city,' Gran said, giving us one last squeeze before letting us go.

'Well, it's only temporary, remember?' Mum said pointedly, glancing at Riley and back to Gran so quickly it might've never happened.

Gran *hmphed* to herself and muttered something that sounded suspiciously like, 'Well, we'll see about that,' but chose not to fight it any further. Besides, she had other things on her mind. She clapped her hands briskly and started barking out the orders I'd been waiting for.

'Now get all that stuff from the car in the house quickly. And don't leave it on the grass. I can't have people thinking I'm hosting a jumble sale out front. The neighbours will start talking about how I don't know how to look after my own home.'

'Is that still what they do for entertainment round here?' Mum said over her shoulder, already opening the boot and handing the first bag to me.

'You have no idea. Sadie down the road forgot to

water the plants under her windows for a week. It was all anybody could talk about. Someone baked a cake because they thought there'd been a loss in the family.'

Mum chuckled. 'Some things never change.'

'Now don't go leaving that bag in the hallway,' Gran called after me as I swerved around her and through the front door. 'Straight upstairs with it. You and Riley are in the one on the right.'

'I can't believe we have to share,' Riley sulked under her breath. Somehow, Gran still heard it.

'You're welcome to sleep out under the tree,' she sang, shimmying into the kitchen where something baking in the oven smelled like heaven. 'I've got blankets and a pillow if you want to give it a go.' Riley glared at the kitchen door as it swung closed.

Our new bedroom for the summer was bigger than both of ours combined back home and looked like it hadn't been decorated since before Mum was born. Riley, her foul mood wafting around the room in waves, claimed the single bed by the window. I thought of protesting, but one look at her face – stuck between eating something sour and disgusting all at once – warned me off it. Maybe now wasn't the time to pick a battle.

'What's with this floral thing?' I said instead, pointing at a strip of paper that sat above the skirting boards and ran around the entire room. 'Oh my God, it matches the curtains!'

'Don't let her hear you bad-mouthing the décor,' Mum warned behind us, blustering under the weight of a large suitcase. 'It's been this way since the eighties.'

'What's that about my curtains?!' Gran's stern voice called upstairs.

'Nothing!' I shouted back, fanning them out to get a better look. 'Just saying how lovely they are!'

Riley sank on to her bed and put her earphones in, closing her eyes and crossing her arms. Even though I'd almost come to expect it now, it still hurt a little to be shut out by my own sister. We'd always been so close. Now it seemed like we were drifting further and further apart.

I sat on my bed on the other side of the room, looking around me and taking it all in. Everything was different, even if nothing had really changed. The bedroom looked the same as it always had, but now it was *ours*, even if just for the summer. I wondered about my bedroom back home, empty and waiting for someone else to call it theirs, and about Lucas and how I hoped he wouldn't make a new best friend while I was gone. With a sigh, I fell back into the pillows, staring up at the ceiling. This was going to be a long summer.

CHAPTER 8

WE'RE DEFINITELY NOT IN LONDON ANY MORE

It took far too long under the sweltering afternoon sun to get all the bags inside the house and where they should be. Gran bided this time by sitting in her armchair and calling out instructions. There was a lot of:

- 'No, that doesn't go there, Camille.'
- 'Bea, could you take this up with you while you're going?'
- 'Get that stuff off the grass before someone calls the council on me!'
- 'Riley, could you fetch my crossword while you're in the kitchen? You're not going to the kitchen?

Well, you're halfway there now so be a sweetheart and bring me a glass of water too.'

We were more than happy when Gran announced she was going next door for a cup of tea, and most likely a gossip, with Miss Hart and Miss Finch. Mum was busy emptying suitcases, which left me and Riley with nothing to do other than explore. Well, we could've unpacked our own bags, but there wasn't much adventure to be had in that.

'Don't be gone too long! Dinner in this house is at five and not a minute later!'

'Yes, Mum!' I shouted back over my shoulder, racing to keep up with Riley and ignoring the tut she gave me when she realized I was on her tail.

We started off up the lane, with houses lined up spaciously on either side. Unlike London, where cars would be bumper to bumper and honking fiercely at each other, there was nothing on the road here except . . . well, us. And bugs. With wings. Lots of bugs with wings. The sun was lazily sinking in the late-afternoon sky. If you stood still and listened, you could hear the chirping of the birds in the trees, and the purr of a tractor out in a distant field. But that was it. A haze of peace and quiet wrapped itself around St Regent's Vale, making my thoughts louder than usual.

I glanced at Riley out of the corner of my eye. She still had her sweater scrunched up around her fists, even though it was really too hot to be wearing more than a T-shirt. Her face was blank, giving nothing away, her eyes floating over well-manicured gardens as we walked on until the village square came into view ahead of us.

St Regent's Vale was basically a collection of streets that unfurled from a cobbled square in the centre. The village hall took up one entire side of the square, and an immaculate church, small and pristine, took up another. On the third side were three shops – a grocer's, a butcher's and a charity shop – as well as the library and the post office. An old-fashioned pub called the Crane in the Sky sat on the final side of the square, squashed between Catherine's Café and Pacey's Bakery, with a fish and chip shop called Thyme & Plaice nestled in the corner for good measure. Each building was painted a shade of pastel so when you looked at them all lined up together, a rainbow of sorts stared back.

As we passed open doors, we finally began to see and hear signs of life – laughter floating through a window, a sneeze from another. One of the shopkeepers gave us a wave, as did the baker and the woman in charge of the post office. An older couple, who had to be even older than Gran, sat under the umbrella of a tree outside the Crane in the Sky. When a small group of adults came streaming out of the church doors, I stopped and took a long look around. 'Are we the youngest people here?'

Sure enough, nobody in sight looked younger than Mum, and they didn't look like *us* either – they were all white. Now I thought about it, it was glaringly obvious and I suddenly felt like I was under a microscope. As those trickling out of the church made their way home, I spotted more than one peering back over their shoulder to take another look at us.

'Maybe they're hiding?' I tried to joke into the silence between me and Riley, but I faltered on the delivery and it landed flat.

I glanced around the square, sure that someone who looked like me would just appear if I searched hard enough, and it was then I spotted a pair of eyes and a messy nest of hair hiding behind a low wall lining the square. I squinted to get a better look, something which has never made any sense to me because surely *closing* your eyes is not helping anybody see more of anything. The eyes blinked as the person they belonged to slowly edged around the wall. It was a boy, short and flustered and seemingly just as intrigued by me as I was by him.

I was about to point him out to Riley when we suddenly heard a cry. It cut through the lazy summer air lingering around the village square, getting gradually louder. The boy's eyes widened, and he scarpered off in the opposite direction at full speed like his butt was on fire.

'What's that?' Riley started off towards the sound, with me so close to her heels I could've been her shadow.

We followed the noise round the corner and down a side street where we found a huddle of kids, maybe half a dozen or so, scattered around in a semi-circle. I breathed a sigh of relief at the sight of people my age, but was quickly dragged back down to Earth by the cry, which had reduced to a loud sniffle.

It was a boy, younger than me and seemingly made up of nothing but snot. He was on the floor, his knees pulled up to his chest so he was as small as possible, his face crumpled by sobs and tears dripping into his lap.

'What happened?' asked one of the older kids, probably

as old as Riley, as he crouched down and put a reassuring hand on the boy's shoulder.

The boy sniffed and tried to open his mouth, but another clipped yelp escaped, and he descended into tears once more.

'We thought you managed to get away,' another girl said quietly. She looked the same age as me, which gave me a thrill despite everything that was happening. She stood next to the older boy, her green eyes identical to his and darting around the street. They had the same dark red hair with a matching patch of freckles splattered over their nose and cheeks.

'Sh-sh-she caught m-m-m-me,' the boy cried, wiping his nose on his sleeve. The kids around him shared a wary look. Riley frowned and stepped in front of me, like whatever had made the boy cry might jump back out at any second. For a moment I forgot to be scared, so elated that a snippet of the old Riley had appeared to protect me. As my big sister, it was kind of her job.

'Come on, Skip, let's get you out of here. You know, in case she comes back.'

The group all hooked a hand around Skip and pulled him to his feet, guiding him away and ducking down another street, out of sight. The girl and her older brother remained, talking in hushed whispers as they walked in our direction. He was tall and thin, with a face that reminded me of a pixie, all dainty and delicate. His ears were on the larger side, glistening with silver hoops and studs. The girl had the same gentle features, her lips pulled upwards so that even though she was clearly scared, she still looked kind of happy about it.

'What was all that about?' Riley asked as they passed.

The boy stopped and weighed us up with a curious stare while his sister did the same.

'New here?' he asked, although it wasn't really a question. Riley nodded. 'Well, welcome, I guess. I'm Ziggy.' He pointed to his sister, who was now grinning with more power than the sun and waving with just as much enthusiasm. 'This is my sister, Emmy. And that –' he nodded back to where Skip and the rest of the kids had just been – 'was something you're best to avoid. I told them she wasn't in a good mood today.'

'Who's not in a good mood?' I asked, looking around as a chill of unknown fear tingled through me.

Emmy's smile almost vanished, although not quite.

'Rita Ruckus,' she said quietly, as if the mere mention of the name could spell bad news for us all.

Ziggy folded his long arms around himself. 'You'll want to watch out for her, unless you want to end up like Skip. Rita's not someone to mess with, especially in summer.' He seemed desperate to leave, but something caught his eye.

'Cool badge, by the way.'

I glanced at Riley, whose eyes widened a little. Pinned to her sweater was one of the rainbow flag badges she'd got from Pride last year. I'd seen plenty of them pinned to her clothes and bags, so I didn't really notice them any more.

Ziggy and Riley shared a smile while me and Emmy just stood there like fools wondering what was going on. I wanted to tell Ziggy that fancying Riley wasn't going to get him anywhere so he should just quit while he was ahead, but he started off up the street again with Emmy close behind. She glanced back when they reached the corner and gave me another wave.

I made a quizzical face at Riley, who suddenly seemed shy after Ziggy saw her badge, but she just waved me off. 'I think that's enough exploring for one day,' she said as if she'd just remembered she was supposed to be in a bad mood. Without waiting for a response, she twirled on her heel and started off back home while I trailed in her wake, hoping my sister hadn't just retreated into herself all over again.

CHAPTER 9

THE WICKED WITCH OF ST REGENT'S VALE

On our first morning in St Regent's Vale, I found myself nestled under my duvet and the wrong way around entirely, my head at the foot of the bed and my feet at the head. For a brief moment, I thought that maybe I'd somehow been transported back to London, or that we'd never left in the first place. I stayed under the duvet for a little while longer, enjoying my daydream that the engines and sirens, which were my usual alarm clock, were just taking a day off, and that Lucas would be knocking on the front door at any minute.

But when I finally popped my head out, the first thing I saw was those God-awful floral curtains. They did nothing to stop the sun from lighting up the room with its soft morning spotlight, but they were clearly not affecting Riley, who was basically a breathing, snoring lump of sheets and pillows. Well, at least she couldn't be in a bad mood if she was asleep.

I sat up, rubbing my eyes and stretching the sleep away. Through a crack in the curtains, I could see the pastel blue of a summer sky, faint and delicate as if it too were waking up for the day. From somewhere downstairs, I heard the whistle of a kettle, cupboards opening and mugs clattering together. And it was at this point that I started to think. Like, *really* think.

We were going to be in St Regent's Vale for the summer, whether we liked it or not. A bad mood wasn't going to change that. If anything, it was just going to make it worse. Riley was obviously still moping about the whole leaving home and missing London Pride thing, and Mum was still treading on eggshells so as not to upset her any further. But that didn't mean that I had to sit around and feel sorry for myself. In fact, I was adamant that I could make this all better, that I could cheer Riley up in some way.

I needed a plan, one that would break the clouds of Riley's bad mood. A holiday wasn't the same without her. When we went to Skegness a few years ago, my favourite part of the trip had been roaming the arcades with her, folded in half with laughter as we tried (and failed) at the dance machine. I wanted *that* Riley back. I just needed to figure out how to reach her, and there was no time like the present to start trying.

I padded over to the door, still in my pyjamas and bonnet, and trotted off downstairs to help with breakfast, my mind firmly set on making things better somehow.

'Morning!' I beamed, bursting through the kitchen door with enough energy to be heard four fields over. Gran jumped and spilled her tea over her toast. Mum banged her knee into the table and swore, her hand flying to her mouth in shock.

'Camille!' Gran exclaimed, swatting Mum's hand with a rolled-up newspaper. 'You can leave that city language where it came from. I won't have my neighbours thinking I raised a potty mouth!'

I swallowed a laugh and pretended to cough instead, hiding a smirk with my hand. Mum getting told off by her own mum? That was something I would've paid to see!

Mum mumbled an apology, grabbing a cloth to clean up the mess. 'What's got into you, Bumble?'

I plopped myself down at the table and grabbed a slice

of buttered toast. 'I'm just excited for my first morning in St Regent's Vale,' I said, slipping a smile on for size but dropping it when I saw Mum frown suspiciously at the sight of it.

'Well, you can put that attitude to good use and come with me into the village this morning,' Gran chirped. 'Apparently I need a chaperone now.'

I'd heard Mum and Gran arguing about this the night before over supper, about how Gran needed to start looking after herself properly. Apparently, she'd hurt her back and needed to be careful that she didn't make it worse. Gran, however, thought Doctor Dill was just being dramatic and wanted to keep her locked in the house so she'd stop complaining about the waiting times.

She glared at the back of Mum's head before pushing her plate away and standing up. She winced and hobbled, trying to suppress a groan as she straightened up. Mum rushed over to grab one arm while I grabbed the other, much to Gran's disdain, and helped her to her feet. Mum raised her eyebrows at me behind Gran's back – point proven.

'Brush your teeth, wash your face and grab your shoes when you're done, Bumble,' Gran murmured as I helped her shuffle towards the study, which had now been transformed into a downstairs bedroom so she wouldn't have to use the stairs. 'And shake your sister awake while you're at it. What time does she call this? It's almost lunchtime.'

'It's ten past eight,' Mum's voice said from the kitchen.

'My point exactly.' And with that, Gran closed her bedroom door.

When I floated back into the kitchen, Mum was humming a song to herself while washing up, doing a funny little dance with her hips. She seemed freer somehow, lighter now that we'd escaped the confines of the city and could breathe the fresh country air.

'Oh, Lucas texted my phone to see if you got here okay,' Mum said, still swaying her hips. 'I've left it on the side so you can text him back.'

It still caused me great stress that Mum thought twelve was too young to have a mobile phone of my own. Apparently I wasn't allowed one until I was thirteen, which just seemed ridiculous to me, but no matter how much I complained, she wouldn't cave.

As I sulked over this, and the fact I was sure Lucas would be having fun without me, I remembered to ask. 'Who's Rita?'

Mum dropped the plate she was washing. It landed in the sink of soapy bubbles, water slopping over the sides and on to the floor.

'Who told you that name?' Mum asked without turning round. Her shoulders were rigid and tense and her voice sounded like the quiver of a guitar string.

'Uhh, someone in the village,' I replied carefully. 'We found this boy crying in the street and when we went over to see what was wrong, some other kids told us it was something to do with Rita? They said we should stay away from her.'

Mum cleared her throat, drying her hands with the towel before finally turning round to face me. She looked nervous, worry lines mapped out on her forehead. 'Well, whoever it was, they were right. Stay out of her way, Bea. I mean it.'

'But who is she?'

'Can you help me with this blouse, Camille?' Gran called. 'My head's stuck in the arm and my arm's stuck in the head!'

'Later,' Mum mouthed, and went off to help.

Somewhat begrudgingly, and with a lot of mutterings under her breath, Gran had given in and climbed into her mobility scooter for our trip into the village. Well, it was more a case of Mum bundling her into it and not letting her back out again until she'd reluctantly agreed that this was the most sensible way to get the stamps and toilet rolls she apparently needed. I say 'apparently' because, at the last count, Gran had twenty-three toilet rolls hoarded in a cupboard, which she classed as 'running low'.

'I'm more than capable of putting one foot in front of the other, Camille!' Gran huffed from the scooter, parked on the path in the front garden. She scowled at the front gate and then at the pavement beyond. But, despite her attitude, I could tell she was relieved to be off her feet. She held on to the handlebars like she was a racing-car driver.

'Well, now you don't have to.' Mum smiled from the doorstep. 'Keep an eye on her, Bea. Don't let her go too fast in that thing.'

'I'm not a child!' Gran yelped. And before she could hear any more, she was off, hurtling down the path and out on to the road. Well, I say hurtling – it was more of a fast crawl, but I still had to put a skip in my step to keep up.

Riley had moaned about having to get out of bed, and no doubt she would be hunkering back down under the sheets now that Gran was out of the way. This wasn't exactly making my plan for cheering her up any easier, but I wouldn't be giving up without a fight. As for Mum, she was planning on setting up a canvas in the garden shed and doing some painting, which made me so happy I could've burst. She hadn't painted in such a long time, what with her shifts at work getting in the way, that I thought she might never pick up a brush again. I'd asked her what she was painting, but she shooed me away and told me it was a secret. So, that just left me and Gran to venture into the village, which was starting to come alive as the sun began stretching its rays over the rooftops of St Regent's Vale.

The buzz of a lawnmower, a stranger to my ears because nobody actually had grass on my street back home, cut through the morning symphony of radios and whistling kettles drifting through flung-open windows. The man in charge of the beast, slightly older than Mum and with what little hair he had left greying, switched the engine off and raised his hand in greeting to us.

'Morning, Sylvie,' the man sang, wiping his hands on

his overalls. His voice was loud, like he'd forgotten that he'd turned off the lawnmower and was still trying to shout over its noise.

'Morning, Jack!' Gran called, slowing down as we passed. 'Fixing up the garden for dear old Wendy, I see. Horrible what happened to her. I'm still not over it. This place will be a lot quieter with her light gone.'

Jack nodded in agreement, suddenly looking solemn. 'Norman's coming up in a few days to sort through the house. You know he always had a soft spot for her,' he said. 'He'll be here once that Pride in London is over.'

I nearly fell over my own legs at that, suddenly alert now London Pride had been mentioned. I tried to hang back to pick up more information, but Gran had started off again.

'I'll rustle him up a cake or something, try and lift his spirits,' she called back. 'God knows he'll need it when he sees his mother!'

And just like that, Gran was off down the lane, humming to herself until we reached the square. The village had been so quiet yesterday, it had almost felt like nobody but the sheep in the fields lived here at all. Now it had come alive with market-stall owners yelling across the way to each other and the waitress in the café calling out for order sixteen (a bacon and egg sandwich with brown sauce and a coffee on the side).

Gran swerved around people's legs, shouting the odd 'hello!' over her shoulder. I trotted behind her, staring about me in wonder.

'All right, Sylvie!' the man behind the counter at the butcher's called out as we passed by. 'See you've got the scooter out!'

'Glad to see those glasses are doing what you paid for, Porky!' Gran hollered back through the door.

'Morning, Sylvie!' a woman with a high-pitched voice and more bags than she could reasonably carry yelped as she jumped out of the way of the scooter.

Gran, a woman on a mission, didn't stop for any of the greetings, zooming from one side of the square to the other and dipping off down a quieter side-street. Here there were several more market stalls, the striped canvas of their roofs softly rippling in the breeze. Gran stopped by one of the stalls and started nattering with the man behind it, and that's when I saw him again – with the same eyes that I'd seen yesterday, this time peeking out from behind a tiny old woman wearing a knitted cardigan and leaning on a walking stick, who I assumed must be his grandmother.

The boy was a little smaller than me, plump with full cheeks and hair that really needed some attention from a brush. But it was his outfit I couldn't take my eyes off. It was like he'd got dressed in the dark. He wore a green T-shirt under a brown woollen vest that had been stitched into a diamond pattern on the front, just like his grandma's cardigan. His shorts were bright orange and stained with mud, torn in more places than I could count. His socks weren't just odd, but completely different kinds, one stretched up to his knee and striped, the other barely above his ankle and a dull pink. He was staring back at me like he'd just seen a specimen in the zoo that he wanted to look at some more but was scared might jump up at the glass. I smiled and waved, more out of awkwardness than anything. He grimaced and raised his hand limply, then seemed to regret raising it at all and quickly dropped it back down to his side.

I was snapped out of the moment by Gran, who had started pulling on my sleeve with urgency. 'Quick, before she sees us!' she hissed, trying to steer me away from the market with one hand and unsuccessfully trying to reverse her scooter with the other.

'Who?' I mumbled, whipping my head around to see who she could be speaking about.

'SYLVIA!'

The booming voice resounded around the street, completely silencing everything else. The people closest to us jumped at the sound, some slinking back into the shadows. The boy with the odd socks looked like he'd seen a ghost, and his grandma didn't look much better for that matter. Gran sighed and muttered something about me not being quick enough to escape. She turned the motor of her scooter off and folded her arms, her face settling into something between a scowl and a glare.

The vendors hid behind their market stalls, the handful of shoppers scattering until the street was almost empty. A cloud had passed in front of the sun, suddenly casting everything into shadow and making me shiver.

And then I saw her.

She was a tall woman, as old as Gran, with short grey hair that had been slicked back and bejewelled spectacles perched on the end of her pointed nose. Her face was stern, her eyebrows thin and sharp. If you asked me, she looked like she'd smelled something deeply unpleasant, or was biting down on lemons that were hidden in each cheek. She walked with the air of a queen, and a mean one at that, marching towards us clutching a black leash in one hand, a regal Great Dane the size of a small lion prowling along by her side. It had pointed ears and a wicked snarl which flashed its razor-sharp teeth. As they got closer, I could hear a low growl, although I couldn't be sure which of the two it was coming from.

'Sylvia,' the woman said again when she was finally upon us, the word harsh and blunt. She looked down on Gran in her scooter with a smirk. Gran just glared straight back up at her.

'Rita. What a pleasure,' Gran muttered, making it clear that it was anything but.

A small chill ran through me at the sound of that name. This was the woman I'd been warned about, and now she was standing right in front of me. As if she could hear my thoughts, Rita flicked her cold, grey eyes in my direction, freezing me in place.

'I'm so glad I've caught you,' she barked, turning her attention back to Gran. 'I have something *deeply* important to discuss with you.' She was holding on to the words for a second too long, savouring each one with a cruel hiss.

'Well, get on with it then.' Gran didn't look impressed or scared for that matter, which was more than could be said for me.

Rita pursed her lips. 'It's come to my attention that you haven't been coming to the meetings for the summer fete recently. In fact, I have it down that you've missed all of them.' Rita raised her eyebrows expectantly, that smirk still there. 'Is there a reason for that exactly?'

Gran didn't waste a second. 'I thought I'd put my time to better use and watch paint dry instead.' The smile briefly faltered on Rita's face, but she recovered quickly, even if the smile now looked forced.

'It's vital that *everybody* attends these meetings. The fete is of great importance to the village of St Regent's Vale. Those who are *not* there risk their own voice not being heard.'

Gran snorted. 'Tell me, when was the last time somebody who wasn't you spoke at one of these meetings? Quickly!'

Rita stuttered, starting words but not finishing them as she searched for an answer to Gran's question. In the end, she settled with clamping her mouth shut into a thin line of fury, her eyes narrowed into slits. The dog growled menacingly but Gran just nodded with satisfaction while I silently wished that she'd just let it drop so we could get home unscathed.

'I'm glad everybody else is having fun over there listening to you plan your little party, but I'm afraid I have other things to do with my time. That paint won't watch itself dry!'

My whole body was so tense, I thought it might suddenly shatter into a million pieces.

'Your smart mouth will get you into trouble someday,' Rita said darkly, leering over us. Her dog, whose gold tag said DOZER, growled in agreement. 'Mark my words, Sylvia. You do not want to get on my bad side.'

I instinctively took a step back, but Gran didn't even flinch. 'Of course. Well, if that's everything?' she said, sounding almost bored.

Before Rita could say anything more, Gran turned the motor of her scooter back on and smoothly circled around her, facing back towards the direction of the village square. 'Lovely talking to you, as always. Have a good day!' she called over her shoulder, and then off she went at the speed of a snail, scooting along as if nothing had happened.

I scarpered after her, but not before I'd checked back up the street to see if the boy had been watching all of that unfold. Once again, he'd completely disappeared. As for Rita? She was glaring after us and, despite the summer's day, it suddenly felt like a storm was swirling over St Regent's Vale.

CHAPTER 10

BERTIE'S STORY

Gran didn't have much to say about Rita Ruckus. In fact, when I asked her about what had just happened, she shrugged it off and gave a little *humph*, like an itchy sweater that she couldn't wait to get off her shoulders. It was Mum who filled in the blanks.

'Ahh, you've met Rita already, have you?' she said tightly, setting down the palette she'd been using to mix paints at the table. She'd been spending time out in Gran's shed with her supplies. 'I meant to tell you about her earlier. That woman's been evil since even I was a little girl.'

Mum slipped into a kitchen chair, cradling a mug of herbal tea. Riley was in the garden, her earphones in to block out the world. Gran was in the living room already, feet up on the pouffe and a crossword in hand.

'You know Rita?' I asked, hopping up into a chair after I'd nabbed several biscuits. I bit into one and tried to make myself comfy.

Mum chuckled to herself, but it was humourless. She paused for a moment, looking out of the kitchen window. 'Everybody around here knows Rita. Her husband owned half the village when I was a little girl, but we always knew it was Rita who ran the show. I suspect they own the whole lot of it by now.'

'Gran doesn't like her all that much, does she?'

Mum shrugged. 'I don't think many people around here do. People with that much power don't always do what's best for everybody else. They just think about what's best for themselves. Rita's no different.'

I nibbled another biscuit and thought this over, picturing the Rita I'd just seen in the village. 'What was she like when you were younger?'

Mum paused, unearthing buried memories. She shuddered at the thought of them. 'Well, if I'm being honest, she was a nightmare. Cally Briggs started the rumour that Rita was a witch after spying on her garden from the woods. She said she saw her doing some hocus-pocus nonsense and reciting a chant from this big, thick book. It seems silly now, but we believed it because we were sure only a witch could be so nasty. Sometimes we'd dare someone to creep as close to her house as they could. One day, Peter Binkley came back in such a state, swearing blind that her eyes had turned red and she'd chased after him with a cane in her hand. We all slept with our lamps on for weeks, scared she'd come after us next.' Mum took a sip of tea, gripping the mug hard enough to crack it. 'She doesn't like kids at all, even though she's got one of her own. Funnily enough, he never comes back to visit – not even at Christmas.'

I frowned because even if she wasn't nice, not having your family around at Christmas seemed quite a lonely way to live. Surely it made Rita sad.

'She's just not a nice woman,' Mum continued. 'She hated me and all of my friends when we were little. She was on our case for years. We lived in fear of doing something to upset her because she wouldn't think twice about cutting a kid down to size. I was just lucky that I had Gran to look out for me, but not everybody was so lucky.'

'What did she do?' I said, mouth slightly open and biscuits now completely forgotten.

Mum sat up a little straighter, memories darting into her mind. 'Well, there was Bertie. I remember Rita had just taken over the post office, as well as all the shops for good measure. That year, old Bertie the postman was turning seventy and we all thought it'd be kind to chip in for something together, make a big celebration out of it for the whole village. St Regent's Vale isn't exactly big, so everybody knows everybody, and everybody loved Bertie. But Rita wasn't having it because she knew that the birthday celebrations would fall on the same weekend as her beloved summer fete.'

She glowered at the mug in her hands. 'It's this thing she throws every year. It's supposedly meant to be about *strengthening community bonds*.' Gran snorted from the living room. 'It's just the Rita show now. Everybody knows it's nothing more than a celebration of herself, and she expects everybody to attend. There's no excuses. Betty Winterbloom gave birth on the same day one year – Rita was so awful to her afterwards that poor Betty ended up moving to another village altogether.'

Mum grimaced at the thought. 'Anyway, Rita was so scared about her big day being overshadowed by Bertie's party that she refused to chip in for a present, and she even refused to let Bertie have the day off to celebrate. In fact, she gave him more letters to post than usual and threatened to have him fired if he didn't deliver them all by the afternoon. Bertie had never missed a day of work in his life. Come rain or shine, he was out delivering the post without a complaint, and he was always so happy and cheerful about it too.'

Mum cleared her throat and adopted a voice that didn't sound too unlike Rita's drawl: 'We can't just grind to a halt for the day to celebrate someone's *birthday*. It's imperative that we continue as normal. Bertie will have to celebrate his birthday in his own time, when it's more convenient. In the autumn, perhaps?'

Gran came shuffling into the kitchen, rubbing her back. 'I knew she was a witch, but that was a low moment even for her. Poor Bertie.' Gran scowled some more, grabbed a new pen from the drawer and hobbled off back to her crossword.

'Did Bertie get his birthday party?'

Mum shook her head sadly. 'He was never one to complain and he tried to tell everybody that it wasn't really a big deal anyway. He retired later that year, and we all chipped in again to plan this huge birthday party to make up for the one he didn't get the year before.' Mum sighed, shaking her head some more. 'He died three weeks before the big day. The party still went ahead – his wife, Eve, said it was what he would've wanted – but it obviously wasn't the same and the whole thing just felt miserable.'

My sadness for Bertie was trumped by my outrage that somebody could be so cruel. I knew I'd had a bad feeling about Rita when I saw her, but this was worse than I could have ever imagined.

'That was the closest anybody ever came to confronting Rita. People were hurt and angry about the whole thing, and there were a few choice words thrown around, but it was mostly done behind her back because nobody had the guts to say it to her face. But I bet you can imagine who *did* say something to her face.' Mum gave a pointed look towards the living room and I giggled. 'Gran's the only one who won't be moved by Rita. Everybody else will do anything she says just so they don't have to deal with the drama if they don't. It's easier that way.'

Mum shrugged and started clearing the table before Gran could complain about a stray biscuit crumb or two. 'It's best you stay out of Rita's way, honey,' Mum said, raising a pointed eyebrow at me in the reflection of the window. 'I mean it when I say she thrives off terrifying everybody around her. Don't give her a reason to single you out.'

'Sure,' I mumbled, pretending I hadn't already thought about various plans to get revenge in Bertie's honour. No doubt Mum noticed the tone, but she chose to ignore it this time, instead glancing out into the back garden, weighing up Riley with a vague smile. I joined her at the window and watched as Riley murmured the words to a song we couldn't hear, her eyes closed, face pointed towards the sun and basking in its glow. Her hands were behind her head, braids splayed out around her in the grass.

'Do you think Riley will be okay?' I asked hesitantly. She'd basically built herself a cocoon, shrugging this hard shell around herself like armour to hide away from us all. Even me. I thought about my plan this morning, to keep positive and upbeat. But now, standing in the kitchen with Mum and worlds apart from my sister, I wasn't sure if it would be enough.

'Of course she will be,' Mum said carefully, not taking her eyes off Riley. I could almost hear the whirring of her thoughts, going around and around in her head. 'She's just got a lot going on right now, and Pride meant a lot to her. She'll be fine. Just give her some space and wait for her to come round.'

This space we were all meant to be giving Riley didn't seem like the best plan of action if you asked me. I mean, it hadn't worked yet, and we'd basically given her enough space to build a castle on. We needed to try something else, something that would make Riley forget about missing Pride. Something that would cheer us all up about missing home and missing Dad.

I didn't know what that something was, but I *did* know it was time to get inventive.

CHAPTER 11

THE GREAT AND LEGENDARY
WHEELIE BIN WAR

'Colour?'

I plopped myself down next to Riley in the grass, determined to get my secret *Make Riley Happy* mission underway. Riley, her earphones still in and eyes closed, didn't hear me, so I nudged her with my foot. Maybe not the best way to get her attention – she nearly jumped higher than the tree itself.

'What are you DOING?!' she exclaimed, her hand at her chest and breathing heavily.

'Just coming to say hello, that's all.'

Riley removed one earphone but kept the other one in. I wasn't sure if this was a good sign or a bad one, or maybe a mix of both, but at least it was something.

'Colour?' I tried again.

Riley sighed and lay back in her bed of grass, closing her eyes again once they'd successfully completed a weary roll. I didn't think she was going to answer, but then she finally said, 'Orange,' with a faraway, dreamy voice.

Well, orange was definitely better than black! I thought of traffic lights and how orange sat in the middle of green and red. Depending on which way it was going, the orange could lead to something good and positive . . . or it could go the complete other way, which would be a disaster. It felt like my sister was balancing on a cliff's edge, swaying towards the red and then the green. Would she fall back on to safe ground or forwards into nothing?

I didn't want the conversation to end there, not now Riley hadn't shooed me away. I plucked another question out of my head at random, picking at a thread on my shorts. 'What do you think of this place?'

Riley opened one eye, suspiciously surveying the greenery around us like she'd woken up there by accident and was seeing it for the first time. 'It could be worse, I guess,' she said, propping herself up on an elbow. 'It's pretty here. And it's so quiet too. It's definitely not London.'

'Is that a good thing?'

Riley shrugged and lay back down. 'I haven't made up my mind yet. But some phone signal wouldn't go amiss.'

We fell into a comfortable silence, Riley humming along to her music while I picked daisies and tried to make a chain. I've never been too good at crafty things like that, though, so I just ended up with a lapful of daisy heads.

'I met that Rita woman earlier,' I said, giving up on my flower jewellery. Riley didn't seem interested, but I was determined to keep trying to reach her and so quickly reeled off what had happened and what Mum had just told me inside.

Riley wasn't too impressed by tales of a local villain, even though she used to love my stories. Talking to her used to be as easy as breathing. Now it was like wading through mud. But I wasn't going to give up. I tried to think of something else since it was clear that Riley wasn't going to steer this conversational ship anywhere other than to the bottom of the sea.

But I didn't get a chance to because just then Riley jumped up, wiping grass from her clothes. 'I'm going for a walk,' she murmured.

I sprang up too, falling into step beside her. 'Where are we going?'

Riley sighed, already putting her other earphone back in. 'I meant on my own. I'll be back for dinner. Later.' And with that, Riley scooted around the house, down the garden path, and off up the road. I watched her go, trying to tell myself that my feelings weren't a little hurt and bruised. My *Make Riley Happy* project was barely off the ground and it already looked to be in danger of blowing up in my face.

Well, to hell with that. I counted to ten, then to twenty for good measure. 'I'm going to explore!' I shouted through the open window. I heard Gran start muttering something to herself about not showing up the family in public.

'Be home by five, Bea!' Mum called.

I waited until Riley was way up the road, her hands dug into her hoodie. Then, without a second thought, I sprinted off after her. If Riley didn't want company, then fine, but I still wanted to know what she was getting up to.

Gran's little cottage sat on the edge of St Regent's Vale. In one direction, the one I'd already explored, was the village itself, a short walk along flourishing, tree-and-cottage-lined lanes. The other direction was something quite different. The neat, meticulous lawns that marked the houses of St Regent's Vale gave way to wild grass and shrubs which had been allowed to grow in whatever entanglement they saw fit.

The hills in the distance rolled upwards and downwards, seeping into farms and paddocks and small patches of woodland. It was beautiful, even if it was tiring work trying to navigate it all. I was starting to regret wearing trainers that certainly weren't white any more after stepping in something I'd chosen to believe was brown paint instead of . . . well, you know.

As I strode along the verge, somewhere between a jog and a brisk walk, I kept close to the trees, watching Riley carefully, hoping to get some new information to help my mission. She didn't seem to be in a hurry, trotting down the road and gently bopping her head to her music.

The end of the lane forked off in two directions. Riley stopped to assess the situation while I slipped into the shadow of a tree in case she suddenly decided to turn round and abandon her walk altogether. But, after a moment of consideration, she took the road to the left, disappearing from sight. I counted to five, then ran after her, reaching the fork in the road more out of breath than I'd like to admit.

The road wound on through the trees, narrow and empty. Riley was nowhere in sight. I sighed, breaking the silence around me. My mission was off to a great start. I carried on walking, hoping that I might just bump into her by accident, but after five minutes, I still couldn't see her anywhere. I muttered to myself, leaning against a rotted wooden fence. The fields all looked the same to me – just large patches of grass with sheep and cows scattered around them. I wasn't even sure I'd be able to find my way back home, which was just wonderful.

'What are you doing?'

I jumped so hard, I fell through a gap in the fence, rolling head over heels down a slope on the other side. I came to a stop a little way down, dazed and confused about how I'd suddenly gone from standing on my own two legs to now looking up at the sun in the sky and . . . a face, peering over me, one that I definitely recognized. It frowned, unsure what to make of my clumsiness. Then it smiled but seemed to think better of it and quickly went back to the frown.

It was the boy from before, the same boy whose eyes had been peeping over the wall, watching me and Riley. He'd changed since I'd seen him at the market that morning – now he was wearing a stripy green T-shirt with long sleeves, and shorts that were trying to be the same colour but were slightly off. He'd wrapped a red belt around himself for good measure. I didn't think I'd ever seen someone dress so ... well, like they didn't care all that much.

The boy blushed and shrugged so deeply his shoulders almost came up over his ears. 'Sorry,' he mumbled. He extended a hand, then saw how muddy it was and blushed even more, whipping it back to his side and wiping it frantically on his shorts. He tried again. The hand was still muddy, but I grasped it anyway and got back to my feet. My knees and legs were just as dirty as his hand, and my shorts were now grass-stained too.

The boy and I locked eyes – his a greeny-blue, kind of like mint ice cream – for the briefest of seconds, but he quickly looked at the ground again as if he'd been electrocuted just by making eye contact. He opened his mouth. Then closed it again. Opened it once more, but nope, it closed again without a word. Well, this was silly, and he clearly wasn't going to talk first, so ...

'Hi, I'm Bea,' I said brightly, thrusting my hand into the space between us. The boy seemed suspicious of the gesture but took it gently all the same.

He frowned again. 'Bea like B-E? Is that your real name?'

I frowned straight back. 'Bea as in bumble bee but not spelled the same. B-E-A. And it is my real name, or I wouldn't have told you it, would I?'

The boy shook his head quickly. 'No! I didn't mean it in a bad way! I just meant . . . it's a nice name, that's all. I haven't heard it before.'

'Oh. Well, uh, it's nice to meet you.' Another silence was threatening to rain down on us, and the boy didn't seem like he was going to do anything about it. Honestly, why was it always down to me to keep a conversation going?! 'What's your name?' I tried.

'Name's Noah,' he said, although it was still more of a mumble and kind of hard to hear. 'Noah Tall, if you can believe it.' He flicked his eyes up off the ground and gave me a wry smile. I giggled, mostly because Noah was actually quite short – just a little shorter than me – and he seemed to relax a little.

'So, what's your deal? I haven't seen you around here before. You're new?' Noah slipped his hands into his pockets and started to walk in the direction I'd been heading. I fell into step beside him.

'My gran lives here. We've moved in with her for the

summer since …' I faltered, not sure I wanted to tell Noah the real reason just yet. I couldn't stand the looks of sympathy when I told someone my dad wasn't here any more. It always changed everything. Sometimes it was just easier to say nothing, so I shrugged instead and carried on, hopping over the real reason like it was a puddle. 'My sister didn't want to come, though, and she's still sulking about it. Well, at least I think she is. She seems to be up to something now.' I have this thing where my mouth just opens of its own accord and runs away with itself. Noah, who didn't seem like much of a talker anyway, didn't seem to mind.

'Who's your gran? If she lives here, then I must know who she is.'

'Her name's Sylvia Gordon but people call her S—'

Noah stopped in his tracks, mouth wide open as if his jaw had completely detached from his face and was trying to go elsewhere. '*The* Sylvie Gordon?' he said and gasped in what I hoped was wonder and not horror. What had Gran done now?

'Maybe …' I answered back, suspicious that Gran had been up to no good. It would be a long summer in St Regent's Vale without a friend, so I wanted to make a good impression.

'Woooooow.' Noah's face was a funfair of astonishment, his mouth fixed into a perfect little O. I tensed, still unsure if this was good or bad. 'That's SO cool,' he suddenly erupted, loud enough to send a bird fluttering away from its perch in a nearby tree.

'Sorry,' he said, blushing a little. 'But just wait until I tell the others!' Noah pointed down the lane and started running, leaving me to trail behind in his wake.

'Wait, wait, wait!' I said, still confused by what was happening. Noah reluctantly stopped, although he was obviously itching to get going. 'What's all this about my gran?'

'Oh, yeah. Sorry.' Noah wriggled on the spot, trying to get himself back under control. 'Well, Sylvie's something of a legend around here. She's the only person in this village who's ever stood up to Rita. They're like, mortal enemies or something.'

I thought *mortal enemies* might be a bit of a stretch. But then, Gran had never been one to hold her tongue. We'd grown up under her orders to always stand up for ourselves, no matter what. Rita might have intimidated everybody else, but Gran wouldn't back down to her.

'Okay, maybe not *mortal* enemies.' Noah interrupted

my thoughts. 'But everyone knows they don't like each other. Rita never backs down to anyone because she doesn't have to – people just do whatever she says because she owns this whole place and if you don't, who knows what will happen? But Sylvie? Rita's never won a battle against her, even the one about the bins!'

Noah had started off up the road again, me floating along beside him. 'The bins?'

'Oh yeah – the Great Bin War a few summers ago. At the time it was all anybody could talk about.'

'All anybody could talk about was ... bins?' I was beginning to think Noah might be losing his marbles.

'You know, the wheelie ones you put outside your house? Sylvie had painted a flower on the side of hers because she thought Mr Wittington across the street was stealing it in the night and—'

I choked. 'Who is Mr Wittington and why was he stealing my gran's bin?'

Noah veered off to the left suddenly, pulling back a large branch to reveal a wooded clearing. A dirt track stretched off into the trees, not appearing to have an end. He nodded encouragingly and started marching off into the woods. I paused, not sure I should be following a stranger, but Noah just bounced along without a care in the world. So, with a shrug, I went after him.

'The wheel on Mr Wittington's bin had gone wonky so when you pulled it outside to be collected, it wouldn't go in a straight line. Sylvie swore blind she saw him swapping his bin with hers in the middle of the night and marched straight over the road in the morning to get her bin back.' Noah giggled at the thought. 'They did this for weeks – Mr Wittington swapping the bins in the night, Sylvie dragging it back in the morning. In the end, Sylvie said enough was enough and painted a flower on the side of her bin so Mr Wittington couldn't steal it any more.'

I grinned at that, hopping over a shallow ditch as we made our way deeper into the woods. *Very clever – nice move, Gran.* 'But what does that have to do with Rita?'

Noah's face was flushed with excitement, like he couldn't wait to get all the words out and didn't quite know where to start. 'Well, when Rita caught wind of the whole flower thing, she went up to your gran's door and basically said she had to remove the flower because it was ... what did she call it? Oh, yeah, because it was an "eyesore" and stood out like a sore thumb.'

I faltered at that, dumbfounded. 'Rita was mad because of a flower? And since when was a flower an eyesore?'

Noah's excitement was bubbling over in earnest now, a bounce in his step. 'That's what your gran said! But Rita said it had to go or else there would be consequences, and when she says that, she means there's going to be trouble. But the next day, when Rita went back to check, there were *two* flowers on the bin. The day after that, there were three, and the week after that I think we counted seventeen flowers altogether.' I pictured Gran's colourful bin, sitting like some kind of rainbow sentry outside her house, and laughed.

'Rita was FURIOUS! But every time she complained and threatened Sylvie, another flower would appear. Anybody else would've just got rid of the flowers and complained about Rita behind closed doors, but your gran just kept painting more.'

The picture of Rita I was sketching in my mind was getting clearer with every story I heard, and it wasn't exactly a good one. But I didn't have much time to think about it right then because I realized we were deeper in the woods than I'd thought. The sun was entirely blocked out by the green canopy above, the light filtering down to us in a green-tinged haze. Left and right, forwards and backwards – every direction looked nearly identical.

'Uh, Noah? Where are we going?'

But Noah wasn't listening. He was concentrating hard, scanning the area around us. 'Aha!' he exclaimed suddenly. He slapped a tree trunk which had been etched with a drawing that kind of resembled a star, if said star had been drinking something funny. Then he carefully counted ten steps forwards.

'We're here,' Noah said proudly. I frowned at the bush he was pointing at, identical to every other one surrounding it.

'Where is "here" exactly?'

Noah reached into the bush and pulled on a branch, revealing a space big enough to clamber through. Blue sky and sunlight beckoned to us through the gap, urging us closer.

'Welcome to the Den,' Noah said grandly. And with a wink, he slipped through to the other side.

CHAPTER 12

THE SECRET HIDEAWAY

Back home in London, our den was pretty much a wasteland. I mean, I've already told you about the patch we'd claimed as ours and how it's really nothing all that special. But even though it's made up of dirt and dust, rotted wood and jagged metal, broken windows and has a sofa that's probably more hazardous to sit on than a pile of pins, what with all the broken springs, me and Lucas love it all the same. It's ours. Our own little escape.

Now, I want you to remember that I said this, because the following might sound like I'm betraying the den I love so much. I'm really not! But . . . well, Noah's den was on another level entirely, and there was no point lying to myself about that.

When we stepped through the hedgerow, we found

ourselves at the end of a large field. The trees we had just come from formed a rugged line right the way down to a fence at the far side. A couple of old and weathered wooden buildings were dotted around, and a house that had no business being so big sat on the opposite side. Noah, seemingly keen to avoid detection, slouched down a little so he was shuffling along the treeline in half a crouch. He pulled on my shoulder to do the same, peering over towards the house for any sign of movement.

'What are we doing?' I whispered, heart in my throat as it always is when I know I'm doing something I shouldn't be. I needn't have whispered, though – the house was so far away that even if the windows were wide open and I were shouting, you still wouldn't be able to hear me.

'We're almost there. You'll see in a minute,' Noah said over his shoulder.

We were edging closer to the nearest wooden building, a good-sized barn that had maybe seen better days but was still in good condition. It was perfectly square, the wood painted a dark red. There were windows near the roof, evenly spaced apart, the white of their frames flaking. The large barn doors were closed, but through a crack in the middle I could hear voices getting louder and louder.

It sounded like they were arguing about something, but I couldn't tell how many voices there were or what they were arguing about.

Three steps away from the door, and now hidden out of sight from the house, Noah stood up straight again and fixed me with a serious look. His eyes narrowed as if they really meant business.

'Now, do you promise to never tell anybody about the location of the Den, the people inside the Den, or indeed anything that happens within the Den?'

I shrugged and nodded, trying not to give away the fact that I was more excited than I was letting on. 'Sure,' I said. Noah assessed me once more, nodded to himself, and stepped up to the barn doors, throwing them open and letting the light from outside pour in.

I'm not ashamed to admit I gasped at the sight before me. The first thing I saw was a wide-open space in the middle of the barn, covered with a huge and inviting rug. There were bales of hay scattered around the space which doubled up as seats, with blankets and cushions strewn over them. Fairy lights had been hung up on wooden crates, casting a warm glow over the Den. My eyes fell on all kinds of other things dotted around the space – a rocking horse that had had its face painted blue, an old, golden birdcage, a trailer with one of the wheels missing, several chipped plant pots and more chairs than I could count, most of them with legs or backs missing.

The walls of the barn were spattered with paint, various drawings brightening up the dark wood. Names had been scribbled and etched, faces had been painted and sketched, and random swirls and whirls had been scattered at will with no real artistic direction at all. To the right, an old, rickety staircase led up to a landing and, through the wooden bars of the banister, I could see more bales of hay, these ones occupied by a small group of kids in the middle of a fierce discussion. Noah started off up the stairs, a bounce in his step.

'Watch the eighth step,' he said, skipping over one of them as he went. 'It's old and cracked and if you fall through and break a leg, I don't know how we'll get you back home without getting caught.'

Caught? Who was going to catch us? And why was being here suddenly seeming like a dangerous idea? Despite the warning bells ringing in my head, a small thrill was flickering, growing with every step I took. And that thrill was joined by my curiosity too, about who owned this place and who those voices belonged to. As I hopped over the step I'd been told to avoid, a girl at the top noticed me from her hay bale and stopped talking. The rest of the voices ceased too, suddenly aware that a newcomer had arrived. One, two, three heads turned as we reached the top of the stairs. My heart did a funny little flutter while my brain started asking questions like, 'Do you have leftover lunch stains on your T-shirt?' and, 'Is there snot clinging to your left nostril?'

'Uh, hey,' I said, raising a hand before realizing waving seemed kind of lame and clamping it into my pocket instead.

'Hey, guys, you've got to meet somebody! You're not gonna believe this.' Noah, clearly comfortable in company he trusted, grinned mischievously, bounding into the middle of the space. 'This is Bea!' There was no immediate reaction other than continued blank stares, so Noah pulled the ace from up his sleeve. 'Bea *Gordon*.'

I opened my mouth to say that my last name wasn't actually Gordon, but, before I could explain, there was a sudden commotion.

'WHAT?!' the girl who'd first noticed me screeched, leaping up from her bale of hay and nearly smacking the boy next to her round the head in the process. I recognized her from the square, with her dark red hair that was identical to her brother's. Emma?

'No waaaaaay,' the boy that she'd almost given concussion said in awe. He was younger than the girl but had the same red hair and freckles, with bushy eyebrows that took up a lot of his forehead. The boy couldn't be older than ten and held the leash of a small dog tightly in his hand. It had a golden-brown coat and a wet nose that was begging to be *booped*. The dog lifted his head up off the floor, looked me over with suspicion, and settled back down to nap once more.

The final boy, who had been nestled in the corner, unfolded himself from a beanbag, stretching out his limbs. He was tall and gangly, his arms and legs not quite moving in sync with each other, as if they were struggling to keep up with him. He had circular glasses perched on the end of his nose and dark, scruffy hair, loose strands of which curled down to rest on his forehead.

'Gordon? As in legend of St Regent's Vale? *That* Gordon?' he asked in wonder, scrutinizing me like I was some golden treasure he'd just found.

Noah nodded so ferociously that I thought his head

might fall off. 'The very one!' he squealed. 'She's Sylvie Gordon's granddaughter and she's gonna be here all summer!'

'Woooooah,' all three of them said in unison, staring at me in amazement. In that moment, I felt almost famous.

With the spotlight burning down on me, I started to feel a little shy, which was a first. The unfamiliar feeling crept around my body, dancing through my arms to the tips of my fingers and warming my cheeks. It felt like I was on the back foot somehow, as if this was a new story that I had to start reading from the middle. So, with three faces staring greedily at me waiting for me to say something, I . . . completely floundered.

'H-h-hello,' I managed. I tried to clear my throat, where that feeling of embarrassment had now settled into a seemingly immovable lump. 'I'm Bea. It's uh, nice to meet you all.'

The girl didn't seem to mind my pathetic greeting and rushed forward to give me a quick hug, shrieking with delight. 'I'm Emily Jones, but everybody calls me Emmy. We kinda already met back in the square? You were with your sister, right? It's so lovely to meet you properly, and to finally have another *girl* in the ranks! It's exhausting being surrounded by *boys* all the time!' She hugged me close again and then pointed to the younger boy. 'You already met my older brother, Ziggy, but this is my little brother, Harry. You can call him Squirt if you want to – we all do at home.'

Harry waved enthusiastically, bouncing on the spot like he might explode with excitement. 'And this is Smudge!' He held the leash up in the air jubilantly. The dog at his feet lifted his head once more at the sound of his name, gave us what I was almost certain was a dirty look, and settled his chin back down on his front paws. I'd never been much of a fan of animals – the only pet I'd had at home was the class hamster in Year Six, and that only lasted a week – but I had to admit, Smudge was pretty cute.

'And that's Robin,' Emmy said.

Robin – the tall, dark-haired boy with glasses – lifted one unco-ordinated arm and flung his hand around in some kind of wave.

'Welcome to the Den,' Emmy went on, dancing back over to her bale of hay, pulling me with her. 'We've never had a new member before!'

'We were going to invite Tilly once but she's such a

blabbermouth and can't be trusted with secrets,' Noah said, crouching down to give Smudge a stroke behind the ears. 'So, it's just the four of us. Well, five now,' he said, beaming.

'Where did you come from?' Robin asked. His voice bounced down low and then shot back up high in an instant. He ducked his head and blushed while Noah giggled.

'London. I've lived there my whole life but . . . we're here now.' I bit my lip, fighting off the blush I could feel heating up my face and hoping nobody was going to corner me with questions I didn't want to answer just yet.

'How long are you here for?' Harry asked.

'Noah said until the end of summer, Squirt,' Emmy quipped.

'But the end of summer could be anytime! The sun's still warm in September. Remember last year when it was warm in the middle of November?'

I gawped at that, because my idea of the end of summer had been August at a push. 'I'm not sure. I guess we'll see,' I murmured. 'So, what is this place anyway?' I looked around at the barn, taking it all in once more. It looked even prettier from above with the sunlight spilling in from the high windows down on to the floor and up the walls.

'It's our top-secret hideaway! Nobody knows about it but us. I don't think anybody even knows that it's here, actually. It wasn't all that exciting when we found it, and I guess it could do with sprucing up a little. It might not be much but . . .' Emmy trailed off.

'It's perfect!' I said, and all four of them beamed at that. 'How did you find this place? Do you own it or something? And who lives in that big house?'

Emmy, Robin and Noah all looked at the floor, guilt written all over their faces. Harry didn't get the memo, though. 'It's Rita's!' he sang, and the others took a sharp intake of breath, their secret now out in the open. It suddenly made sense why we'd had to creep from the trees to the barn like spies on a mission.

'This barn belongs to Rita?' I asked warily, looking from one guilty face to the next in search of an explanation.

'Well, technically yes, it does belong to Rita,' Robin confessed into the silence, still staring at the floor.

'But she never uses it!' Emmy butted in, defensive and almost trying to convince herself as well as me. She eyed the barn doors, like now the secret was out, it might scarper up to the house to tell Rita.

Noah sighed and shrugged. 'Okay, yes, this is Rita's barn and yes, she lives in that ginormous house. But she has so many huts and barns on her land that she never uses half of them. Apparently she doesn't even use all of the rooms in her house! This barn has been abandoned for years now, and she'd never come down all this way. Not unless she had reason to believe that there were four kids and a dog who had made this their second home . . .'

He looked up at me, almost begging me to keep the secret. The others joined his silent pleading, all big puppy-dog eyes that Smudge would've been proud of. But they didn't have to do much convincing. After everything I'd heard about Rita in that one day alone, I was already set to go against her in any way that I could, even if I hadn't met her properly yet. So what if Noah and the gang had made a den out of one of her barns? If she had so many that she couldn't use them all, then she wouldn't miss one of them.

I grinned at my new group of friends. 'The secret's safe with me.'

CHAPTER 13

BE GAY, DO CRIME

We passed the rest of the afternoon playing card games while Smudge continued to snore, ignoring our existence until he either wanted a treat or a wee. It really did seem like he was living the life of Riley (not my sister – apparently this is a phrase, although I don't know who that particular Riley is meant to be . . .).

It turned out that Noah, Robin and Emmy had all been friends for years and had been in the same class since they were toddlers. Harry had only started tagging along with the group after Emmy's parents insisted that she take her little brother with her whenever she went out with friends, something that she still didn't seem overly happy about. But their parents had bought them a dog last Christmas, which had softened the blow, and so Smudge was the last recruit before I'd come along.

They were all excited to have me there with them, although I couldn't be sure if this was to do with me or their adoration for Gran. They asked questions at a million miles an hour, like where I went to school and who my friends were back home and how I liked it in St Regent's Vale even though I hadn't been there for all that long. The questions only stopped when Noah jumped up with a stick and started speaking in a low, mysterious voice, announcing himself to be the Lord of the Vale and Defender of the Den. Robin immediately jumped up on to his own hay bale, nearly falling off it in the process. He grabbed a stick and thrust it into the air, declaring an invasion on the barn.

'They do this all the time,' Emmy said with a roll of her eyes, but she was grinning as she watched Robin, Noah and Harry roleplay some great war, clashing sticks and zipping around the barn with pretend armies on their tail.

'It's really not a bad place, you know?' Emmy mused as we looked down over the final cries of battle. 'St Regent's Vale, I mean. I've lived here all my life and I can't imagine living anywhere else. It's small and there's not always a lot going on, but the people are nice and kind, and a place is only boring if you let it be.'

'I don't think it's a boring place at all,' I said back, thinking of all the wide-open spaces and secret hideaways like this that you could never get in London.

'What about your sister? You said she didn't really want to come in the first place?' Emmy took her eyes off the battle and faced me, crossing her legs.

'Yeah, well, she had her reasons. Riley had plans this summer to do something important, something that means a lot to her. She's just upset that she can't do it now.'

Emmy thought this over. 'She can't just do it here instead?'

'It's not that kind of thing. It's ...' I thought of how best to describe Pride. 'It's a rainbow-coloured adventure.'

When the battle was over, we sprawled out over the barn, Harry riding the rocking horse while the rest of us lazed around in the hay bale seats, sharing bottles of water and cupcakes that Emmy had packed in her rucksack. I told them all about Riley properly, about how she wanted to go to Pride again this year but couldn't. I hesitated to tell them why Pride was so special to us, though. They were all so nice and kind, but I couldn't start taking my walls down now, so I skipped around that part.

Harry was excited by the sound of an adventure of any kind, and Emmy was pretty taken with the idea of rainbows and balloons and glitter. Robin was aghast at the thought of dancing in public but admitted that the whole thing did sound pretty fun, while Noah just wanted to investigate London Pride properly since my explanation of drag queens and outfits made entirely of feathers just raised more questions than it answered.

The sun had started to slip down in the sky when I realized I was definitely, without a doubt, going to be late home. 'What's the time?!' I shrieked, leaping up on to my feet.

'It's almost seven,' Robin said.

'I'm in *so much* trouble,' I groaned. 'I need to get back for dinner.'

Noah offered to show me the way back, since we'd need to go through the woods again and I'd only get lost if I tried it by myself. 'Come back tomorrow!' Emmy called as we started racing out of the barn.

'For sure,' I called over my shoulder, wondering if I'd actually be able to or if I'd be grounded for the next week.

I couldn't fight the smile on my face, though. Even if I was late and most likely in a whole heap of trouble, the summer in St Regent's Vale was suddenly beginning to look up.

'WHERE HAVE YOU BEEN?!' Mum erupted before I was even through the front gate. She'd been hanging out of the window, looking frantically up and down the street for any sign of me.

'I'm sorry, I'm sorry!' I held my hands up in surrender as I scurried to the door and inside the house, ready for all hell to break loose.

'What time do you call this?!' Mum looked ready to explode, her face scrunching up in rage. Her blood was boiling so hot, I was surprised that smoke didn't start hissing out of her ears.

'I lost track of time,' I muttered. I'd escaped into another world for the afternoon, one where I'd finally made some new friends. Now I was quickly crashing back down to Earth as I realized just how much trouble I was in.

'It's almost midnight,' Gran scowled, leaning around the kitchen door.

'It's not even eight o'clock!' I argued back. Big mistake, but you should know by now that my mouth just opens whether I give it permission to or not.

Gran fixed me with a look that could melt an iceberg and continued muttering to herself as she made a cup of tea – something about manners, I thought I heard, or lack thereof.

'And where's your sister? Is she not with you?' Mum looked over my head and out of the front door, scanning the darkening lawn for Riley.

'She's not back yet?' In my excitement at discovering the hideaway, I'd completely forgotten that following Riley had been my actual mission from the beginning. Where had she got to?

Mum paced the hallway in fits and starts, throwing ideas out into the air one by one before rubbishing them and starting over. Gran had taken up residence in her favourite armchair by the window, continuing her muttering as she craned her neck this way and that, glancing up and down the street for any sign of Riley.

'Letting them kids run riot like this in the city, and now look!' Gran said to nobody in particular. Mum, from behind the wall in the hallway, pulled a face in

Gran's direction and leaned out of the front door once more.

'WHERE HAVE YOU BEEN?!' Mum exploded for the second time that evening.

I braced for impact, wondering how much trouble we could possibly be in now Riley was home.

'Riley? What's wrong?' I frowned, my heart beating faster as I peered around Mum to see my sister hurrying up the path. The evening light made it hard to see her properly, but as she stepped out from under the shadow of the tree, her tear-stained face came into focus and my heart sank.

'N-nothing,' Riley stuttered, even though we all had eyes that told us otherwise.

'Well, something's the matter, so spit it out,' Gran said firmly. She might've sounded stern, but there was a look of concern on her face all the same.

Riley stood in the hallway, hugging herself with the folds of her hoodie. Her head was down so that her hair fell over her face. 'I saw that woman,' Riley finally said, so softly that for a moment I wasn't even sure she'd said anything at all.

'What woman?' Mum asked gently.

Gran huffed and folded her arms. 'I bet I can guess who she's talking about. And it shouldn't take you three tries to guess as much either.'

Mum paused before the penny dropped, then quickly enveloped Riley in a hug, pulling her in close and holding her tight. Gran tutted to herself and went to pop the kettle on.

'Who's she talking about?' I asked, pushing my way between Mum and Riley so I could join the hug too.

'That Rita woman,' Riley sniffed, and my body went stiff. Mum held Riley at arm's length to get a proper look at her before steering her into the living room, fussing around her until Gran came back with steaming mugs of hot chocolate, topped with cream and mini marshmallows for good measure. She settled back into her armchair, even more alert than before.

'So, what happened?' she asked, her narrowed eyes searching Riley's face.

Riley cradled her mug and sighed. 'It was silly. I don't know why I'm crying. It just took me by surprise.' She shook her head to clear her thoughts, sitting up a little straighter. 'I went out walking to try and explore this place and I must've taken a wrong turn or something.

I was kind of lost and didn't know the way back when I saw this big house.' Gran scowled some more, and I understood why – it didn't take a genius to know who that house belonged to. I'd seen it with my own eyes only a few hours before.

'I just thought I'd ask for directions or whatever, so I stopped and knocked, and that woman answered.'

'*Witch* would be a better way to describe her. Woman is far too kind.' Gran huffed. Mum gave her a pointed look and placed a reassuring hand on Riley's knee to continue.

'Well, it was hot, and I'd taken my hoodie off and wrapped it round my waist. I didn't really think about what I had on underneath ...' Riley trailed off, like she does sometimes when she doesn't know what to say next.

'It wasn't one of those tops that show off your tummy, was it? God forbid that woman of Satan see even a flash of skin on one of the hottest days of the year.'

'Mum, *please*,' Mum sighed. Gran glared at the wall but kept her mouth shut. 'So ... what did you have on?'

Riley put her mug down by her feet and shrugged into her hoodie, disappearing for a few seconds before she re-emerged. I burst out laughing by accident, but I was even more surprised to hear Gran giggling to herself as well. She read Riley's T-shirt and fell into fits of hysterical laughter, slapping her thigh. She had to take her glasses off to rub the tears from her eyes. Riley half-smiled, and so did Mum, although she tried to hide it.

Riley was wearing one of her favourite T-shirts, a Christmas present from Travis and Rue. It was white and at least one size too big, which was very Riley's style. Emblazoned on the front in a swish of pink were the words: 'Be Gay, Do Crime'.

Mum was the first to recover, clasping her hands together in thought. The rest of the laughter died down too, although it took Gran a minute to get herself together and she was still chuckling to herself.

'Well, what happened with Rita?' Mum asked gently, trying to piece together what had upset Riley so much.

Riley shrugged, biting her lip hard. 'Nothing really, it was just . . . well, she definitely didn't like the T-shirt. I didn't think it was such a big deal, but the way she was going on about it, you'd have thought I'd thrown a brick through her front window. I tried to explain that it was just a joke and that it wasn't serious, but she wasn't having it.' Riley shook her head and took a deep breath, collecting herself. 'It was nothing I couldn't handle. It was just a shock, that's all. I wasn't expecting to be attacked just for wearing a stupid T-shirt.'

Mum pulled Riley in for a hug, rubbing small circles into her back and telling her it was okay. I crossed my eyes and stuck my tongue out at Riley to make her laugh. When I looked over at Gran, though, she was no longer chuckling to herself. Instead, she was glaring out of the front window, where a shadow was beginning to emerge.

Rita had arrived.

CHAPTER 14

AN UNFRIENDLY VISITOR

There was a moment where everything seemed to freeze. Mum went tense and rigid, which scared me even more than Rita's silhouette. If *she* was nervous, then this was bad. Really, really bad.

'I'll handle this, Mum,' Mum said to Gran, jumping up from the sofa before Gran could get halfway out of her seat.

'Don't you dare, Camille. Get back in here,' Gran muttered. Her jaw was clenched tight, anger and rage painting every line on her face.

Mum hesitated by the living-room door and that was enough for Gran to hobble up and put a firm hand on her wrist. Mum sighed, and I knew it was because she sensed trouble, but she stood back and let Gran pass.

Riley sank back as the unmistakable silhouette of

Rita made its way up the garden path. From the way she walked, all upright and official, I could tell that she wasn't happy. It was still light outside, but the shadow of Rita and the great oak tree in the garden were threatening to engulf our house.

Gran whipped open the front door as Rita raised her hand to knock. I peered out into the hallway to see a shocked Rita, her eyebrows halfway off her face. She recovered quickly, smoothing out her blazer and clearing her throat. Behind her, across the street, a curtain twitched, the silhouette of two heads appearing in the window.

'Good evening, Sylvia,' Rita said. There was an edge to her voice, and it was slightly higher than before, tight as a snake that's coiled and ready to pounce.

'I wouldn't call it a *good* evening,' Gran retorted, hands on her hips.

Rita acted as if she hadn't heard and nodded into the house. 'May I come in for a second? It won't take long. I'd just like to discuss . . .' She made to step inside the house, but Gran moved and blocked the door.

'Anything you have to say can be said from right there,' Gran said, as sour as a fizzy sweet. Rita looked like she'd been slapped across the face, or that she might burst into flames at any moment. I couldn't quite tell, but either way it wasn't good.

'As you please,' she almost spat. 'I'm here about a girl I believe to be your granddaughter. Riley, is it? Well, she appeared at my front door earlier all a dither, *claiming* to be lost. I not only found her on my property rooting around in places she shouldn't be, but also wearing a T-shirt that said ...' Rita paused, swirling the words around her mouth and, judging by her expression, finding them bitter. '*Be Gay, Do Crime.*'

Rita levelled the words at Gran as if they were weapons, sending each one, crystal-clear and sharp, out into the air. 'Now, had I not caught Riley pottering around my garden, then who knows what she would've got up to. But I think we should have a talk about not only her lack of respect for private property, but also her encouragement of breaking the law.' Rita peered around Gran. 'Maybe she can also join the talk, and we can come to some sort of agreement on how best to proceed. Hopefully, a worthwhile punishment will teach Riley some much-needed manners.'

Rita looked expectantly at Gran. I couldn't see Gran's face, but I was sure it would be casting some kind of glare that would melt the average person to nothing more than blood and bones.

'Are you finished?' she said simply, as if Rita had been delivering the news that it might rain tomorrow. Rita's eyes narrowed.

'Sylvia, I must insist that y—'

'Let me tell you something, Rita. If you *ever* make one of mine return home crying again, I'll be sure to return the favour. You might be big and clever upsetting a teenager, but I can guarantee between us two women, it won't be me who cries first. Riley and Bea are new to this village, and so long as they're here, they're under my watch. So, any problems you have in future, you bring them straight to me. You might have scared the rest of this place into submission, but I'll be damned if you're going to do the same to my family.'

'Sylvia . . .' Rita tried to butt in, but Gran waved her words away with a flick of her hand.

'Riley was lost and looking for directions. As this village's busiest body, I'm surprised you weren't there with a map and torch to help show her the way. It sounds to me like there's a completely different issue here altogether.'

Rita stepped back, her mouth now slightly open as she

fought to think of something to say. But Gran shook her head and breathed a humourless laugh.

'Now, if you don't mind, I had planned on having a *good* evening before you arrived at my door looking for trouble. So, if that's everything . . .'

Before Rita could say otherwise, Gran stepped back and slammed the door hard. When she turned around to face the three of us, who were now in the hallway and not even trying to hide any more, she looked as if nothing had happened.

'Right then – anybody for some food? You must be starved!' And off she shuffled into the kitchen.

'I can't believe that just happened.' Riley was curled up at the foot of her bed, a book open on her lap but the pages unread since we'd escaped upstairs after dinner and closed the bedroom door. She'd been staring holes into the rug instead, thinking hard. I didn't want to interrupt, knowing full well she'd have something to say when she was done assessing whatever was running through her mind. When she finally opened her mouth, I immediately sat up straight, wrapping the duvet around me.

'All of that had nothing to do with me being in her garden. She saw my T-shirt and just ...' Riley shook her head, her shoulders sagging. When she spoke again, her words were deflated too. 'It's not fair. Some people just expect you to stay in this little box, and the moment you step out of it, the moment they figure out something about you is different, they want to squash it. I just don't understand why some people can't let everybody else live their life the way *they* want to.'

Riley scowled into her lap, her face still faintly marked with the tears she'd cried earlier. It made me hate Rita even more, and every other person in the world who'd ever think of making my sister feel like this just because of who she was. Riley was right – it wasn't fair, not one little bit.

Riley heaved a sigh and climbed under her duvet, the book in her lap falling to the carpet with a soft thud. I didn't know what to say. I'd been thinking for so long about how to make things better, how to cheer Riley up so we could both enjoy the summer, but so far, I'd achieved a grand total of absolutely nothing.

'I just want to go back home.' She said it so gently, I could've mistaken it for my own imagination. But then Riley pulled the duvet up over her head and disappeared.

I sat still, unsure what to do. I could leave her alone and let her ride her feelings out. That's what Mum and Dad would say to us when we were sad – that it's best to lean into how you're feeling and go with it rather than pull away and resist, because that can make things worse. But we were sharing a room and I couldn't just sit there knowing she was right next to me and not do anything.

I shimmied out from under my duvet and padded over to her bed, flicking up one side of Riley's duvet and slithering underneath it. It was a single bed, so it was a tight squeeze and I could've fallen out of it at any moment. But we hadn't done this in a long time; not since Riley had got older. We used to hide under our duvets like they were armoured forts and share our secrets where Mum and Dad couldn't hear us. It made me feel like a grown-up, especially when Riley started secondary school and would tell me about all the goings-on. I'd missed our little fortress.

Under the duvet it was warm and stuffy, especially with two of us, but Riley didn't complain. In fact, I could've sworn she even smiled slightly.

'I made a new friend today,' she said quietly. 'Remember that boy in the square? Ziggy? He's gay too. He saw my badge and found me on Instagram. He said he thought I could use a friend. I guess he was right.'

If Ziggy was anything like Emmy, then maybe that was just what my sister needed – a ray of sunshine to brighten her summer. I explained about meeting my new squad of friends too, although I conveniently left out the part about the barn and the hideaway, even if I knew I could trust my sister with pretty much anything.

We talked about everything else: home, St Regent's Vale, Rita, and all of the other things we could think of. It felt like we'd gone back in time, and that my sister was maybe stepping out of the shell she'd hidden away in. Of course, I had to nearly ruin it by asking a question I knew I should've kept to myself.

'Do you think we'll ever go back home? Like, *home* home?' I didn't want to look at Riley's face and see that she'd disappeared again, but I braved a peek and saw her mulling the question over instead. Her eyes were a little watery, but she bit down on her lip.

'I don't know. But if we don't, then … I guess we'll just make a home somewhere else.' Riley scrunched up her nose and grimaced, then shrugged and nestled down into her pillow, her eyes slowly closing. I took that as my cue and hopped out from under the duvet, bounding over to my own bed and settling down into my nest. Riley reached out a hand and switched the lamp off, plunging us into a darkness only broken by a pool of moonlight by the window.

I could feel sleep pulling at me, but I had one more question, one that had been flitting around my mind ever since Mum sat us down at the kitchen table to tell us we were leaving our home.

'Riley?' I said into the dark. It took a moment, but she eventually hummed sleepily in reply. 'Do you think Dad's still with us?'

A middle-of-the-night silence, still and delicate, laid itself between us. Maybe she'd fallen asleep. But then she shuffled, and I heard her release a wobbly breath.

'I hope so, Bumble. I really hope so.'

CHAPTER 15

A RAINBOW ON THE NEWS

I have to admit I'm not really a fan of the news. I know adults love to tune in and pretend they understand what's going on, but for the most part, the news just seems to be full of misery and gloom. There's never anything good or happy on there. It's all global disasters and how politicians plan on upsetting our lives next – that's what Mum says anyway.

Dad would read the newspaper every morning with a slice of toast and a cup of tea going cold on the table as he groaned and moaned about one thing or another. Mum would roll her eyes and tell him that he shouldn't start the day off on such a bad note, but Dad would always shoot back that it was important to stay informed, even if the news was terrible. I was definitely on Mum's side when it came to this particular matter.

Anyway, the reason I'm telling you about the news is because Gran, just like Dad, would catch up with the daily goings-on every morning. She'd start with a newspaper in the kitchen while the kettle was boiling, humming and tutting to herself every couple of seconds. There'd even be a shake of the head at the particularly bad stuff. Then, once she had her tea and had successfully finished assessing the misery, she'd shuffle on into the living room, switch on the TV (this huge bulky thing that looked like an ancient metal box belonging to a different world) and catch up with the news in visual format instead.

Nobody else was allowed to touch the TV remote in Gran's house anyway – 'Do you pay the electricity bill and TV licence?' she'd say – but in the morning, we all had to keep the noise down so Gran could concentrate on whatever woes were happening in the world. However, on this particular morning, it wasn't all doom and gloom.

'London Pride will be the biggest one yet, so say the organizers and the newly appointed Director of Communications, Rupert Boon,' the news anchor said and, at exactly the same time, every head in the living room shot up. Out of the corner of my eye, I glanced at

Riley, who was now paying more attention to the morning news than she'd ever done before. I mean, it wasn't exactly difficult, considering she was usually buried in her phone, but now she was sitting forwards, breathing a little quicker.

On the screen, the picture changed from inside the newsroom to overhead images of London. It was strange to see the city I called home from a completely different perspective, up in the clouds and looking down over everything. It made me think of Lucas, back home and enjoying his summer without me. I wondered what he was doing, and who he might've found to replace me.

The skyscrapers of London looked as magnificent as ever, glinting proudly in the sunlight, and even the River Thames had upped its game for its TV cameo, the usual steely greys of its tides now brighter and rippling with rainbows.

Wait. Rainbows? In the Thames? I frowned and sat forward like Riley for a better look. And that's when I realized that what I thought was a colourful River Thames was actually a video of last year's Pride, the one we'd been to together. A stream of never-ending people trickled down a street, moving as one big mass, every colour of the rainbow winking up at the camera. I wondered if, somewhere in that crowd, was us.

'That's a lot of people,' I breathed in wonder. There had to be thousands. Tens of thousands. Maybe even hundreds of thousands.

Mum looked a little uneasy, flicking her eyes between the screen and Riley with a look of vague worry. Gran was nodding along with the news anchor, who was interviewing this Rupert Boon person and asking questions that I couldn't really hear because my heart was beating in my ears and I didn't know why. Riley was captivated, mesmerized even, as the pictures changed and showed London Pride over the years. In many ways, the pictures showed a Pride that was completely different from the one I'd been to. The hair was cut into bowl shapes and the outfits were, to be honest, hideous. But one thing was exactly the same – everybody looked so happy to be there, together. Each picture and video that appeared was a snapshot of joy, a moment of happiness frozen in time. The feeling I'd had that day, one I hadn't felt since, swirled through me, warm and fuzzy, just like magic.

'London Pride will be bigger than it's ever been before,'

Rupert Boon was saying proudly. 'There will be more diversity and representation, more events and occasions. And, of course, the parade itself this weekend, which promises to be the gem in our London Pride crown. You really don't want to miss out this year. It will be the pinnacle, not only of the UK Pride scene, but of every Pride event around the world.'

Me and Mum flinched at exactly the same time, both of us casting furtive glances in Riley's direction. She was staring at the screen so intently that I thought it might explode. Her eyes were watering but, as the interview drew to a close, the trance broke and she quickly blinked away her tears. She stood up, gave the image of London Pride on the screen one last look, and then disappeared out into the back garden. And just like that, we were back to square one.

Mum made a job of cleaning up the breakfast plates and bowls, even though she still hadn't finished her own. I wondered if she'd try and talk to Riley. There was no doubt that this weekend was going to be thoroughly miserable, what with London Pride happening hundreds of miles away. I wondered if her best friend Elmina, or maybe even Taylor, the girl Lucas was sure was Riley's girlfriend, would be going without her. That'd surely make things harder. But maybe once it was over, no longer taunting her from a distance, she'd be able to move on. I hoped so anyway.

Before I could think about it any further, there was a knock at the door. Gran, probably anticipating a rematch with Rita, waved me back down on to the sofa and tottered out into the hallway to answer it.

'Morning, Mrs Gordon!' I heard a familiar voice sing. 'Is Bea at home? Harry! Get off the grass! Smudge, you too! No, don't pee there! Sorry, Mrs Gordon!'

'You're the Pacey-Jones girl, aren't you?' Gran said as I appeared behind her. Emmy nodded eagerly. 'I know your parents, and your grandparents actually. Lovely shortbreads they have in that bakery of yours. I was always begging your gran for the recipe.'

Emmy beamed at that. 'I'm sure I could find it for you, Mrs Gordon! If I do, I'll bring it straight over!'

'Please, call me Sylvie. Mrs Gordon was my mother-in-law and, God rest her soul, I hope to be nothing like her.' Gran shuffled away from the door, winking at me in the process. 'Thanks for making friends with the shortbread girl,' she whispered and toddled into the kitchen.

'The shortbread girl?' I asked, stepping out into the sun and offering my hand to Smudge. He gave it a look like it might be poisoned, then bounded off after Harry, who was pretending to be a superhero with laser-beam guns for hands.

'Oh, yeah.' Emmy blushed. 'My family own Pacey's bakery in the square. It's been in our family for generations. It's almost as old as St Regent's Vale. One day I want to work there properly and run the place, just like my parents.'

The idea of owning a bakery was almost more than I could bear. The thought of all the doughnuts and pastries and cakes you could ever want, right there at your fingertips? It sounded like paradise, if you asked me.

'I brought some cupcakes for today,' Emmy said as if she'd read my thoughts. 'I made them myself.' She blushed again as I inspected the cakes nestled in

her rucksack, sitting alongside bottles of water and juice. 'That's if you still want to come to the Den,' she whispered. I nodded frantically before she'd even finished the sentence.

'I'm off out!' I called into the house, hoping I wasn't about to get pulled up for being late the night before. But Mum didn't seem to mind, too preoccupied with moving her painting supplies out to the shed.

'Don't be late home this time. Five on the dot, okay?' she called.

We set off up the road, Harry and Smudge cantering along ahead of us, so I took the opportunity to tell Emmy all about Rita's unexpected arrival the night before. Talking about it reignited my rage over the whole thing. I was still furious that she'd made Riley feel that way. Emmy listened thoughtfully as I spoke. She didn't even seem surprised. In fact, she gave a grim nod, like she'd been expecting something like that to happen.

'That's just Rita, I suppose,' she said sadly. 'I know it doesn't feel like it, but it sounds like Riley got off lightly. Poor Tabatha Tick still has nightmares from when she tried to sneak on to Rita's porch for a dare. Rumour has it you could've heard Rita from nearly a mile away she was so mad. And when Ziggy dyed his hair green, she nearly passed out with rage on the spot. She doesn't like anything to be *different*.' Emmy sighed. 'You just don't want to get on the wrong side of her. Staying out of Rita's way is the best you can do.'

It was advice I'd already heard but it seemed a little rich coming from Emmy and the others. 'You've literally built a den at the bottom of her garden, using one of her own barns! That's not exactly keeping out of her way, is it?'

Emmy winced. 'Yeah, well, there was a lot of discussion about that when we did it. We needed somewhere to get away from the village, and Noah's grandma started hosting board game afternoons, so we couldn't hang around there any more. It took us nearly a whole summer to pluck up the courage to check out the barn, and we only did it because Robin was absolutely certain he'd heard Rita bragging about having so much space that she didn't even use half of it.'

'And how did Robin overhear that?' I asked as we reached the fork in the road and started off towards the woods.

'His mum cleans Rita's house. She spends six hours

a day there during the week, trying to clean everything exactly the way Rita likes it. If she doesn't do it perfectly, Rita takes the money out of her wages. She says it's a valuable life lesson that you only get paid for what you've earned. It's little things like an ornament facing the wrong way, or a speck of dust on a book that she doesn't even open. She inspects the house every night and if she finds something that she doesn't like . . .'

Emmy let the pointed silence fill in the blanks. 'She knows Robin's mum will never quit because she can't afford to. Like I said, she's a horrible person.'

We climbed through the gap in the bushes, Harry and Smudge bounding off towards the barn in the same crouching position. Noah had showed me. Me and Emmy paused, both of us looking up towards Rita's house. It really was huge, way bigger than was necessary for just two people and a dog.

'I hate her,' Emmy whispered, still half in the bush for cover. 'I don't hate anybody if I can help it, because everyone has something good about them if you look hard enough, right? But Rita? I'm not so sure. She's hurt so many people in this village just because she can.' She shook her head and started off towards the barn, where

Robin and Noah were already waiting, Robin mending one of the broken chairs while Noah perched on the rocking horse, watching.

'That has to be a new record for getting on Rita's bad side,' Noah said, all in a fluster after I'd told them what had happened. 'We should've warned you sooner!' Today he was wearing a green and pink patterned woolly vest over a fluffy orange jumper. It made me do a double-take when I first saw him, but Emmy didn't even seem to notice.

I shrugged. 'Gran sorted it out. She didn't even give Rita a chance to get past the front door. I think we'll be fine.'

Robin had begun fiddling with a string of fairy lights that wouldn't turn on, holding a screwdriver between gritted teeth. He lifted his head slightly. 'Be careful, Bea. She's a nasty piece of work. Just ask my mum,' he said out of the corner of his mouth.

'Anyway, what's this about London Pride? You said it was on the news? I wish we could see it for ourselves. It sounds so magical!' Emmy clutched her hands to her chest and swayed dreamily.

'It's happening this weekend, which means Riley's going to be even more miserable than before.' I shuddered.

'I can't think of any way to drag her out of this mood. Not unless we just jump on a train and go to London ourselves without telling anybody.'

Noah nearly fell off his perch at that. Even Emmy looked a little concerned. I held my hands up in surrender. 'It was a joke!'

'Why isn't there one here?' Harry called, running laps with Smudge who looked like he was three seconds away from admitting defeat and flopping down on the ground to sleep.

'One what?' Robin called, now satisfied that the fairy lights were working again and tucking away his screwdriver with an affectionate pat.

Harry stopped running and looked at us. He shrank back a little, shrugging. 'If there's a Pride in London, why isn't there one here too?'

'Because it wouldn't be London Pride then, dummy,' Emmy snorted. 'It can't be *London* Pride if it's not in London, can it?'

Harry shrugged and went back to playing with Smudge, but something was nagging at me. *It can't be London Pride if it's not in London, can it?* My mind wasn't even in the barn any more. It was back in Gran's living room this morning, watching Rupert Boon and the pictures of London Pride.

It will be the pinnacle, not only of the UK Pride scene, but of every Pride event around the world . . .

'Bea? Are you okay?' Noah swam slowly into my vision and I was back in the barn. His round face was full of worry and concern, and it only got worse when I started grinning.

But I couldn't help it. Every adventure starts with an idea, and Harry might've just had the best one yet.

CHAPTER 16

AN ADVENTURE STARTS
WITH AN IDEA

No sooner had the seed of my new idea been planted in my brain, it started to blossom at an alarming rate, shooting off in every direction and stretching its branches further and wider. It was already as much a part of me as my arms and legs. All I could think about was Riley. She'd been a shell of a person for long enough and I knew I had to do something. Maybe this was it.

I've never been good at keeping secrets, so I tapped my foot, I bounced on the spot, I walked around in circles, determined to keep my body busy and my mouth shut while I figured out the best way to tell the others. After all, I'd definitely need their help. But Emmy beat me to the punch.

'You've got something on your mind,' she said, nudging me with her foot and bringing me back down from the clouds for a moment. I smiled and shrugged but Noah was inspecting my face once more, inquisitive and curious. He leaned in closer, as if he'd be able to hear my thoughts if he listened hard enough.

'What is it?' he asked, when that didn't work. Robin put down his notepad that he'd been sketching on and waited expectantly. Even Harry was sitting still for once.

'Well,' I started, unsure how to even say it. Then it just came tumbling out. 'I was thinking about what Harry said and, well, why *can't* we have a Pride of our own? Right here, in St Regent's Vale?'

Harry gave Emmy an 'I told you so' smirk. She screwed up her face at him before turning back to me. 'Go on . . .' she said, cautious but curious.

I shrugged. I didn't know the first thing about London Pride other than that it was a place my sister felt at home, and a place where everybody who went seemed to be happy. I didn't know how it was put together, how it was planned, how much money it would cost to even get the idea off the ground. But they were all branches of the tree I was choosing to ignore. We could cross those bridges when we got to them. For now, I just needed backup.

'Well, if Pride happens in other places, why can't it happen here? It doesn't have to be as big or as glamorous as London Pride, it just has to be *something*.'

Emmy looked unsure, but there was a glimmer of – was that excitement? – twinkling in her eyes. Harry was beaming and brimming with enthusiasm. Robin had raised a single eyebrow and cocked his head to the side, no doubt carefully weighing up the idea and all of its tentacles. But Noah was shaking his head, slowly at first and then more decisively.

'What's up, No?' Emmy asked.

Noah stuttered and started, swallowed, and then tried again. 'Rita will *never* let that happen. You know she won't! We'd need her permission to go ahead with it in the first place, and who's going to ask her? Because I'm *definitely* not. She'll say no, and that's the *best* scenario we could hope for. And aren't you forgetting something?'

Emmy looked back blankly, but Robin understood straight away. 'The summer fete,' he said in a low rumble. Noah widened his eyes as if to say: 'Duh!' Emmy grimaced as the realization dawned.

'That summer fete is her pride and joy. She'll never let anything overshadow it.' Emmy sighed. 'People have moved their entire birthdays and celebrated them in autumn just to avoid clashing with it.'

I thought about Bertie the postman, and of my sister, returning home in tears after what Rita had said to her, and it just made me double down on the idea harder.

'And we should just back off and be miserable because Rita says so?' I blustered, trying (and failing) to keep my emotions in check.

'Well … yes,' Noah said simply. 'That's the way it's always been and the way it will always be. Going up against her is a recipe for disaster.' He shook his head firmly once more. 'Nope, I'm not doing it.'

I could feel my bottom lip beginning to pout and bit down on it hard. I wasn't going to look like a sulking toddler in front of my new friends. Well, not if I could help it. 'What is this stupid village fete anyway?' I grumbled.

Emmy jumped down off her hay bale, walking around the barn in small circles. 'It started off as a day like any other, except there were more market stalls and people usually dressed up in their nice clothes. But then Rita took the reins and made it all about her, of course, and now it's not really the same. People start preparing for it in *March*, making sure everything's just how Rita likes it. Even my parents – they start baking cake samples weeks in advance.' Emmy shook her head. 'The fete was meant to be for the whole village, but now it's just for *her*.'

Robin also hopped up, although he slightly overestimated it and nearly toppled over. 'Think of it as a funfair,' he said once he'd righted himself. 'But without the rides, the games, the flashing lights and everything else.'

'So, a funfair without the fun then.' I huffed, folding my arms and then quickly unfolding them when Robin grinned at my stroppiness. 'Just think about it! It doesn't have to be on the same weekend, or even in the same month. We find out what date the fete is and just throw our own Pride later, so they don't clash. How can Rita be mad at that?' I could hear the plea in my voice but I just couldn't let this idea go. And, knowing it would likely irritate Rita was only making me want to do it more. It felt a little like payback for what she'd done to Riley, and to everybody else for that matter.

'Do you even know what we'd need? To make this happen?' Emmy was mulling something over so hard that she'd stopped wandering about the barn.

I grimaced, not wanting to look like I didn't have the slightest clue what I was talking about. But the truth was, I didn't have a clue, and I didn't even know where to start.

'Well, we'd need a million balloons, for a start. And like, rainbow things. Flags and stuff. Oh, and floats!' I tried desperately.

Noah looked grumpier than I'd ever seen him. 'Oh, all right then! I'll just get the float out of the garage and the rainbow flags down from the loft!' he said sarcastically. 'No, no and no. I'm staying out of Rita's way, and you'd all be wise to do the same.'

Suddenly, there was a big bang. We all jumped a foot in the air, our heads whipping around to look at the barn doors in terror. Noah had gone from standing on his own two feet to leaping into the arms of Robin, who caught him before he could even register what was happening. Emmy giggled at the sight of Noah being cradled like a baby in Robin's arms while Noah and Robin both turned the colour of ripe tomatoes.

We all crept towards the doors, me leading the way with Emmy on my tail. Harry was in the middle, then Robin, and finally Noah, who appeared to be fighting the urge to turn and flee in the opposite direction. I cracked the barn door open slightly and peered outside, ducking low so the others could see over my head.

At first, I couldn't see anything out of the ordinary, just the fields and the trees and the tractor and . . . wait, a tractor? It was rusty and red and sitting a little way up the field. When I looked closely, I could see smoke pouring from the front, great wafts of grey that surely couldn't be healthy. A man I'd never seen before came walking around the side and Noah and Emmy gasped in unison.

'It's Roy Ruckus, Rita's husband!' Emmy hissed for my benefit. 'What's he doing out here?'

We watched as Roy Ruckus slapped the tractor on the side, then on the front as if he hoped that would magically fix it. He was clearly muttering to himself, but we were too far away to hear what he was saying. Whatever it was, he didn't look happy.

'Maybe he'll just go back inside?' Robin didn't sound like he believed his own words. Noah shivered next to me, definitely three shades paler than usual.

'What if he comes over here?' he whispered, trembling.

'He won't, they never use this barn,' Robin said, his usually cool and casual voice all tight and edgy. 'I know they don't – Rita told my mum that they don't use any of the outhouses over by the trees, just the ones next to the house. And there's nothing in here they'd need anyway. So just relax. He won't come ...'

We all inhaled at exactly the same time, holding our breath as one. Roy Ruckus had abandoned the tractor, but instead of walking back towards the house, he was coming straight towards us.

CHAPTER 17

HERE COMES MR RUCKUS

The five of us fell into a heap on the barn floor as we rushed away from the door, a tangle of arms and legs and quiet shouts.

'We have to hide!' Noah squeaked, looking dangerously pale as he got shakily to his feet. His entire body was vibrating with terror. Harry looked like he was about to burst into tears at any moment. Emmy had jumped into high gear, sweeping up cushions and blankets, frantically trying to hide any evidence that we'd been here. Robin tried to tear the fairy lights down but ended up accidentally wrapping the wire around his feet and crashing into a pile of crates instead.

Once we'd retrieved Robin, we all scrambled up the stairs and crawled over to the windows, slowly raising our heads up over the sill to peep outside. Mr Ruckus, dressed up in his best wellies and hunter's cap, hadn't seen us yet, but he was still marching in our direction looking like he might breathe fire at any minute. He stopped at a small shed and poked his head inside the door, shrugged, and carried on towards our barn.

'We're so dead,' Robin whispered.

'We're not gonna make it out of here alive,' Noah confirmed with a whimper. It seemed a little dramatic, but then I thought of Rita and decided maybe it was a possibility after all.

Mr Ruckus was so close now that I could see his wrinkled face, squashed in on itself with half a scowl fixed across his jaw. Wisps of white-grey hair had been cut so short he was almost bald, and his beard had been trimmed with such precision that it could have rivalled any of the front gardens in St Regent's Vale.

'What's his deal? Please tell me he isn't as bad as Rita,' I said in a quiet voice as Mr Ruckus stopped to inspect his watch.

'Not as bad, but definitely not far off,' Emmy whispered back.

'He *is* married to Rita, after all,' Robin added. 'The only reason he gets off lightly is because Rita is meaner than the devil and nobody else can compete.'

'We need to hide!' Noah repeated, now trembling so much that his teeth were chattering.

'He might not even come in here,' Emmy tried, but as if he'd heard her, Mr Ruckus started towards us once more. He was close enough now that we could hear his mutterings through the window.

'Quick!' Noah whisper-yelped, scrabbling for the hay bales in the far corner and diving behind them. Harry picked up Smudge and bolted after him, followed by Robin, who nearly barrelled through the hay bales instead of jumping over them. Emmy grabbed my hand and yanked me towards the opposite corner, pulling me behind a stack of crates and wrapping a blanket over our heads.

The door below creaked open and there was silence.

Nothing moved.

There wasn't a sound.

And then there was a footstep.

It was heavy and foreboding, hitting the ground with a thud. It was followed by another and another as Mr Ruckus entered the barn. I counted them, trying to track where he was. There were five and then silence, as dense as fog on a winter's night.

Another footstep.

Then nothing . . .

And then Smudge. He quietly whined, only for a split second, but it was enough. In the silence, it sounded like a puppy orchestra. I heard Harry and Noah frantically try and quieten him, but it was too late. The footsteps had started again, this time coming for the stairs. Emmy's hand was clammy in mine as we gripped each other tightly, panic now clamping down on us.

The first stair creaked. Then the second and the third, each footstep bringing us closer to our inevitable doom. My heart was starting to beat so loudly that I thought it'd give us away, each beat telling Mr Ruckus exactly where we were.

He was on the fourth step. The fifth.

There was a *whoosh* in my ears like a wave crashing on to the shore. What would happen if he found us? *When* he found us? Would we become a story that others would be told to warn them away from Rita and her husband?

Mr Ruckus was on the sixth step. The seventh.

Not being able to see what was happening was

unbearable. It was making the panic worse. Carefully, I reached for the blanket over our heads and peeked out. He was there, mere steps away from us. The scowl on his face was furious, a shark that had smelled blood in the water.

He took one more step, on to the eighth. And then ...
CRASH!!!!

Mr Ruckus yelped and then disappeared entirely from sight with an ungodly shout, as if a trap door had opened up and swallowed him whole. He landed on the barn floor with a *THUD*, wood raining down around him.

'Rotten barn,' he muttered, rage twisting his words into ugly sounds. There was a lot of groaning (okay and swearing too) as Mr Ruckus got back to his feet and wiped himself off. Then, still grumbling to himself, he left and headed back off up to the house, slamming the barn door behind him.

We waited in silence for ten seconds ... twenty seconds ... an eternity. Nobody wanted to be the first to check that Mr Ruckus had really gone. What if he was just testing us, waiting for one person to move before he jumped back out and gathered us up? Had he *really* gone back to the house? Or was he right outside, waiting?

I took another peek, carefully at first, and then with less care as I confirmed that Mr Ruckus wasn't still in the barn with us. I sidled out from behind the crates and up to the window, peering out over the fields. Mr Ruckus had just reached the house, disappearing around the side of it.

'It's safe,' I said with a sigh of relief. Emmy's head popped up immediately. Robin and Harry also stood up from their hiding spots, scanning the barn to double-check the coast was clear. Noah, of course, was the last to reappear, slowly emerging as if he didn't believe we'd really managed to escape our doom. He was so pale I was starting to think we might have to call an ambulance. There'd be no way to hide *that* from Rita and Roy.

'That was a close one!' Harry whistled, already back to normal as if nothing had happened. He started chasing after Smudge, who was darting about the barn, completely oblivious to the fact that he'd almost got us into the world's biggest trouble. It was hard to be mad at something so cute, though.

'Well, that settles it then, doesn't it?' Noah said with a single nod.

'Settles what?' Robin frowned.

Noah pointed at the barn doors with a still-trembling finger. 'See, it's too dangerous. We're already playing with fire. Case closed.'

I saw his point, but I couldn't let go of my idea so easily. Noah might've been terrified of Rita but he didn't know what it was like to see his sister almost completely switch off, the light in her dimming until it had nearly faded away entirely.

'How about this?' I said, not quite sure where my train of thought was going but aware that I needed to keep Noah from shutting the idea down completely. 'We do some research, figure out what we'd need to do, and then we can make a decision after that. Maybe we'll reach a dead end, and maybe this whole idea will just seem silly once we've read up on it. But . . .' I shrugged. 'I can't just give up without trying first.'

Emmy put a reassuring hand on my shoulder. 'That can't hurt, can it, Noah? We just look into it and nothing else. But like Bea said, we won't know unless we give it a try.'

'I'm in,' Robin said, offering me a high-five. 'That old witch won't scare me.'

'I want to do it!' Harry said, although I wasn't sure he knew exactly what he was signing up for. Smudge gave a tiny yap, his tongue lolling out of his mouth.

'I think that means yes too,' Emmy said with a grin. 'Noah?'

We all turned to Noah, who was refusing to look any of us in the face. He ran a hand through his hair, somehow making it even messier than before.

'No,' he finally said with a grim look. 'No, I won't do it.'

Even though the others had all said yes, I felt my shoulders sag with defeat. Noah was the reason I'd made these friends in the first place, and I didn't want to do this without him.

'I won't do it. I'm sorry, but I won't.' Noah looked in Emmy's and then Robin's direction. 'And you know why.'

Before anybody could say anything else, Noah shuffled down the stairs, hopping over the broken one, and bolted out into the field, leaving the rest of us looking at the empty space he'd left behind.

CHAPTER 18

THE PERILS OF EAVESDROPPING

I didn't see Noah after that. Not for a few days anyway, although it wasn't for a lack of trying. On my morning trips into the village with Gran, I kept an eye out for Noah and his grandma, hoping I'd see him peeking out from behind somewhere, but I had no luck, even when I asked around.

Porky, the butcher, a jolly man with a white moustache and a round belly, hadn't seen sight nor sound of Noah. Neither had Catherine, the owner of the café in the square who always seemed to be balancing plates of scones and jam in her hand while wearing a jam-stained apron. Miss Hart and Miss Finch, the two old ladies who lived next door to Gran and ran a tiny florist's around the corner, offered some hope when they said Noah had come in with his grandma not fifteen minutes before. However, they got into a heated argument about the positioning of a sunflower pot for Rita's fete before they could tell me anything more.

Emmy said she'd seen him once, although only because she'd taken it upon herself to go and knock and say sorry, a box full of muffins in her bag as a peace offering. What she was apologizing for, I wasn't sure. I'd asked what Noah meant about Emmy and Robin knowing why he was so reluctant to take part in our plan. But Emmy and Robin just shrugged awkwardly and mumbled something about asking Noah instead, which was all well and good but, like I said, Noah was nowhere to be seen.

I was baffled about how I could have accidentally hurt Noah's feelings with my grand idea. I ran through the moment, over and over, looking at it every which way to try and make sense of it all, but whichever way I saw it, I was left utterly confused. But another worry soon came into focus – before I knew it, the weekend would be upon us, and somewhere a million miles away, London was gearing up for Pride.

As soon as I woke up, I knew something was wrong. The birds were chirping, the sun was shining, but there was something missing. Then I realized that the usual rhythm of Riley's breathing was absent and, sure enough, when I rolled over to check, she wasn't there. Her bed was perfectly made as if she hadn't slept in it at all.

'Where's Riley?' I tried to ask casually as I bounded into the kitchen, failing to keep the panic out of my voice. Mum seemed just as uptight as me, tapping her foot against the kitchen-table leg and chewing her lip instead of the toast in front of her. Even Gran was sitting up straighter than usual, her hands clasped around a mug of tea.

'She's already headed out for the day,' Gran murmured, raising an eyebrow in the direction of the empty seat next to Mum. 'In quite a hurry too.' Gran pursed her lips. Mum was too lost in her own thoughts to even know I'd come into the room until I plonked myself down at the table. She gave me a quick peck on the cheek and busied herself making a fresh mug of tea, her first having gone stone cold.

'Was she okay?' I asked cautiously, tiptoeing around the subject like it was a stink bomb that could go off in our faces at any time.

'Well, she was up before lunchtime, so what do you

think?' Gran quipped, but she shrugged and sighed. 'Miserable as sin, but to be expected if she really wanted to go to that thing you all went to last year. She'll be fine by Monday when this is all over.' I wasn't sure I believed that, and I didn't think Gran believed it either.

I got washed and dressed, picked out a bright top and dug out my rainbow badge that was buried at the bottom of my backpack from last Pride. We might not be there, but that didn't mean I couldn't celebrate all the same. As I pinned it to my front and saw it glinting back in the mirror, I felt a wave of emotions break over me, threatening to submerge me altogether. I bit my lip and scrunched up my face, trying to push it all back down to where it'd come from. When I was satisfied the tears were safely at bay, I opened my eyes and found Mum watching me from the doorway.

'What's your colour today, Bumble?' she asked, perching on the side of my bed in paint-splattered jeans. No doubt she was getting ready to go back out to the shed.

I mulled it over, still not entirely sure I could risk speaking without the walls I'd built inside myself breaking down completely. I clenched my fists by my side, just to make sure. 'I guess ... grey? But the kind of grey that feels like it's hiding another colour behind it, like a cloud or something.'

Mum nodded, leaving a space of silence for me to continue like she always did when we had a serious conversation. 'I didn't know I'd miss Pride like Riley. If Dad were still here, we'd have gone just like last year and it would've been the best day ever all over again. And I miss him. I really do. I think about him all the time, every day, and sometimes I feel like he's not that far away, that he's watching over us or something.' I felt more tears coming but quickly pulled them back, taking a few breaths to steady myself. 'But it's also started to feel like there's a little bit of hope, that everything might be okay in the end. That there might be some sunshine behind that grey cloud.'

It was Mum's turn to cry, and unlike me, she wasn't embarrassed by a few tears. 'I know it's hard for the both of you, and I know this weekend would've meant a lot. There's nothing I can really do or say to make it any better, but I promise you that as soon as we can, I'll take you both to Pride and we'll have a day just like last year.' I looked at the floor, wondering if I should tell Mum about my idea of making Pride closer than she'd think. But she didn't seem to notice.

'What colour are you feeling today?' I asked instead.

Mum pointed down at her jeans, splattered with more colours than I could count. 'A rainbow colour, of course,' she said, letting out a shaky laugh. 'I'm sure Riley's going to be out distracting herself today. She says she's got a new friend – Twiggy or something.'

I snorted so hard I thought my lungs might come out through my nose.

'It's Ziggy, Mum.'

She frowned, then seemed to remember that I might be right. 'And you've got some new friends too? I saw Emmy's mum when I tried out the yoga class in the village hall. She said you've been getting on like a house on fire. So, you get out there and have yourself a good day and try to forget what's happening back at home.'

She was right. There was no use moping over something I couldn't change. Being sad all day wouldn't magically transport me to London or throw me back in time to last year's Pride. It wouldn't bring Dad back. But what I *could* do was go and see Emmy and Robin and Harry and Smudge, figure out how to convince Noah to come back and help us, and start planning how to bring the end of the rainbow closer to home.

Emmy lived in a spacious house close to the square, with intricate and precise shrubs standing proudly in the front garden. There were rows of flowers framing the path leading up to the door, swaying gently in a summer breeze that seemed to be exclusive to Emmy's house. The front door was adorned by two big plants that were basically trees, and a knocker made of solid gold sat in the middle. It was clear that Emmy's family weren't exactly short of money.

I stood in the cavernous kitchen with Robin as Emmy zipped around the island, stuffing pastries and bottles of water into her rucksack. My eyes roamed over the gleaming marble countertops where vases of gorgeous flowers bloomed. Several cakes were sitting on the island, all lined up in a row, baked to perfection.

'Mum and Dad are at the bakery this afternoon trying out more samples for Rita's fete,' Emmy said, nodding to the cakes. 'Harry and Smudge are at the neighbour's house, and Ziggy's probably in his room, as usual.' She tutted softly to herself, mumbling something about finally being free of her brothers. 'Ready, then?'

As we stepped out into the hallway, which was the width of a road itself, two voices floated down from upstairs. I paused when I realized one of them belonged to Riley, and crept closer to the bottom step as Emmy and Robin did the same.

'Do you think you'll go next year?' Ziggy was saying. I already knew what they were talking about, even if we'd missed the beginning of the conversation.

'Definitely,' Riley replied. 'The only reason I'm not sneaking there today is because I'd have to hitch a ride to the closest train station, and there's no way I'd get away with that. My gran's got eyes all over the place, I swear.' She sighed. 'And I don't want to worry them any more than I already have.'

I pretended I didn't see Emmy and Robin glance at me and instead focused really hard on the staircase.

'You think they're worried about you?'

There was a pause so long that for a moment I thought my ears had stopped working. But then there was a shuffle and I heard Riley clear her throat.

'I don't want to worry them or anything,' she said, her

voice laced with tears. 'I just don't know how to get out of my own head. It's like I can feel something pulling me down and stopping me from being myself. Inside, I'm screaming at myself to act like I did before all of this happened, to be sad about it but to let myself move on. But I just can't do it.'

I didn't want to listen to this. It felt private to Riley and something I shouldn't hear. But I couldn't pull myself away, even if I tried. My sister hadn't opened up like this in so long. Even with this awful tremble creeping into my cheeks, I couldn't turn away now.

'My little sister has been a rock this whole time. I know she's been sad too, but she'd never show it. She's stepped up into the role that I should've taken. I should be looking out for her, making sure she's okay. Instead, it's been the other way around. Sometimes I can't look at her because I'm so embarrassed that I haven't been there for her when she's needed me the most and I—'

A clipped sob broke off the rest of the words and I heard Ziggy move across the room, telling Riley it was okay and to just cry it out because maybe that was what she needed.

I wanted so desperately to run up those stairs and hug my sister tight. I wanted to tell her that I was all right and that she hadn't done anything to be embarrassed about, that she hadn't done anything wrong at all. That I was still her sister, no matter what.

But Mum and Gran were right. Riley would come to us when she was ready. Even though it broke a little piece of me to not run up those stairs, I knew I'd have to wait. In the meantime, I knew exactly what I had to do. My big sister had been there for me through everything – looking out for me when I first started at King's Garden, delivering fresh snacks to the sofa when I fell out of the tree I'd been climbing with Lucas and hurt my ankle. Now it was my turn to do something for her. Riley deserved to have the best Pride ever, and I was going to make sure that she got it.

CHAPTER 19

THE SECRET SUNSHINE PROJECT

The library in St Regent's Vale was older than the three of us combined and doubled. The front of it had been painted a pale shade of blue, its windows a crisp white with small flowerboxes underneath. The door was flung open to invite anybody inside, the smell of old and new books wafting out into the street. It wasn't very big by any stretch of the imagination, just a little bigger than the downstairs of my house back in London, but it was crammed from wall to wall and floor to ceiling with books of all kinds, piles of them leaning precariously one way or the other.

'Morning, Mr Tim,' Emmy sang as we stepped inside. Robin raised his hand in a wave, already veering towards a stack of comics sitting by the counter. 'We just wanted to use the computer, if that's okay?'

We'd decided that a computer away from home was best, so we wouldn't get caught making our grand plan. Hearing Riley had cemented in my heart that we *had* to do this, and thankfully, Emmy and Robin had agreed. It was Emmy who'd suggested the library, mostly because Mr Tim apparently knew how to mind his own business.

Mr Tim was older than most of the books in the library but packed with just as much spirit. He jumped out from behind the desk, a bright grin welcoming us in. 'How lovely to see you, Emily,' he said in a deep, warm voice that sounded like it knew every fact in the world. 'And, of course, you too, Robin. A new Batman just came in. I've popped it behind the desk for you.' Mr Tim winked, pulling out a shiny cover from where he'd been sitting. Robin nearly fell over himself to get at it.

'Is this a new friend?' Mr Tim's eyes came to rest on me, a gentle smile making me feel at ease and like I could tell him anything.

'This is Bea – she's visiting her gran, Sylvia Gordon.' Emmy stepped aside and kind of ushered me forwards, so I smiled and said, 'Hello.'

'Ahhh, Sylvie!' Mr Tim said, and for the thousandth

time I wondered what Gran had been up to all these years in St Regent's Vale. 'She has a particular fondness for classics, but don't tell her I told you that she also enjoys a romance novel from time to time too!'

Mr Tim laughed to himself and scooted back round to his side of the desk. 'A computer, you say? I'm afraid someone's using it at the moment, but he's been back there for some time, so his hour is almost up. I'm sure he won't mind you going and giving him a nudge – I was surprised you weren't on his tail when he came in!'

Emmy whipped her head around, nearly falling into a stack of books as she took off into the library, pulling me along with her. 'Thanks, Mr Tim!' she called back over her shoulder, Robin on our heels with the Batman comic safely tucked under his arm.

The only computer in the library was old, grey and bulky with a keyboard that had a few letters missing from years of brushed fingers. It sat at the back of the library around a bend and tucked away in a tiny nook. When we rounded the corner, I knew who I'd see.

'You'll have a hard time blending in with that orange scarf on,' Robin quipped, making Noah jump so violently that he nearly knocked the whole computer off the desk.

He quickly closed whatever he'd been looking at and turned around, flushed and a little breathless. He refused to look at any one of us, instead eyeing up the spaces in between like he was planning an escape route.

'Hey, Noah,' Emmy tried as gently as she could, but it was no use. Noah mumbled something about needing some fresh air and all but ran out of the library, his orange scarf trailing behind him.

Once again, I was left bamboozled. What had I said that was so seriously wrong that Noah could barely stand to be in the same room, never mind talk to us? I just wanted to know so I could right the wrong and bring him back. I missed him. The group didn't feel the same without him there, but for some reason, nobody wanted to give me any answers.

'What's got into him?' I tried once more, taking his seat at the computer and peering back at the others. 'I know he doesn't want to help with the idea or anything, but does that mean he can't speak to us at all now?'

Robin made a chore of sitting on the floor and opening up his comic with a barely audible, 'I dunno,' that made it clear he knew the exact opposite. Emmy blushed and shrugged, budging up next to me on the chair.

I shifted a little so we were sharing half each. 'There's something going on that I'm not allowed to know, right?'

Emmy squirmed but eventually nodded. She shrugged with a sigh, then tried to smile through it, pointing at the computer. 'So, where do we start?'

I wasn't necessarily offended by the secret – it was more that I hated being kept in the dark about anything. But, if Noah needed time, then that's what I'd give him.

I grabbed the mouse and opened a new internet tab, frowning when I saw that the page I was looking for was already loaded on the screen. Noah hadn't shut it down properly. I looked at Emmy, who made a small noise as her eyes widened. Robin jumped up to look over our shoulders, peering at a screen filled with colour.

'I guess we don't have to look far then,' he murmured.

Pictures of Pride stared back at us, a collage of colour bursting off the screen. It was exactly how I remembered it and a thrill jolted through me as I leaned in to get a better look. There were crowds of people lining the streets as floats glided by, moments captured like magic in a bottle. There were arms and balloons in the air, banners and flags and confetti for good measure. Emmy gasped every time she saw a new photo, struggling to contain her squeals of joy and excitement.

'So cooooool,' Robin marvelled, basically climbing over Emmy's head to point at a bunch of men clad in black clothes and straddling motorbikes. Their chest hair had been adorned with glitter to match their sparkling beards (which made me burst out laughing when I saw Emmy's shocked face) and balloons had been tied to the back of their bikes.

'How do we start figuring out how you make your own Pride, though?' Emmy wondered. She looked warily over her shoulder, like Mr Tim would be standing right there marvelling at the bikers with us.

I pondered this and tried typing 'HOW TO MAKE YOUR OWN PRIDE' in the search bar. The page refreshed after a few seconds with a bunch of different results.

'I don't think this is quite what we're looking for,' I said, clicking on one website that promised we could make our own LGBTQ+ flag in eight easy steps.

'Well, not so fast!' Emmy grabbed my hand to stop me closing the page. 'We'll need to know how to make our own Pride flags, won't we? They were in almost all the pictures! It can't hurt to take some notes.' Quick as a flash, she dug out a notebook and started jotting down the steps, giving herself a satisfied nod once she'd reached the last one.

'We should give our plan a name, don't you think?' Emmy mused, chewing on the end of her pen.

I thought about the colour I'd told Mum I was feeling earlier – a grey, just like a cloud that was hiding something behind it. Something like . . .

'How about the Secret Sunshine Project,' I said, and Emmy nearly cheered. She wrote it down in the front of the notebook, making it official.

Through pages and pages we scrolled, each one giving us tips for one thing or another, but none of them telling us exactly what we'd need to put together a Pride of our own. By the time our hour on the computer was nearly up, I was feeling a bit deflated. Call me a fool, but I'd kind of thought . . . well, that it'd be a little easier.

'We just need to think positive, or else the whole thing will come down in flames,' Robin murmured, biting down on his lip as he concentrated on doodling out ideas. 'I mean, it can't really be that difficult, can it?'

I was about to mutter something under my breath about

how maybe this was a silly idea after all when a sudden, stern voice sent the temperature in the library plummeting.

'George!' it spat, and I knew immediately that Rita had just arrived. Emmy's face wore a mask of panic and Robin dropped his pencil, leaning back into the wall like he was hoping it would conceal him.

'Rita!' Mr Tim squeaked, the deep and warm voice I'd heard when I first walked in now gone. 'What can I do for you?'

'I need the computer. Immediately. Mine's doing some funny swirly circle thing and I don't have time for any technological nonsense today. We have a fete to prepare for. I'm quite sure you shouldn't need reminding of that.'

The breath I'd been holding seemed to explode out of me all at once. Emmy scrambled our things into her rucksack and began creeping along the wall, peeking her head around the corner. With a panicked wave to the two of us, she quickly crawled out into the open, ducking behind a large bookshelf. Robin didn't need to be told twice, grabbing my hand and yanking me along with him. But his legs misjudged the instructions his brain had given them, and he toppled behind the bookcase instead, kicking over a pile of books in the process. We froze.

'Must be ... the wind,' Mr Tim murmured, even though there wasn't a breeze to speak of. If his voice got any tighter, I feared it might give out altogether.

But Rita didn't seem to notice, her arms folded across her front and a blazing look on her face. 'I said I need the computer, George! Have you lost use of your ears? I haven't got all day, *some* of us have got places to be! We don't all just sit around reading books.'

'Of course,' Mr Tim stuttered as a flame of anger steamed through me. Mr Tim didn't seem like he'd hurt a fly, and yet here was Rita, storming in like unwanted rain and making demands without so much as a please or thank you. What happened to manners?!

Peeking through the books, we saw Mr Tim shuffle towards us, his face pale. He spotted our eyes between the stacks and hurriedly put a finger to his lips, before gesturing to the computer for Rita.

'Anybody would think you hadn't heard of a duster before, George,' Rita said in disgust, staring down at the desk as if it carried fleas. Mr Tim hurried back to the desk and returned with a cloth, wiping down the surface and almost bowing when Rita took her seat.

'You can leave me be now. You've proved yourself quite

useless enough already. Your hovering about my shoulder is as helpful as a wasp in summer. Maybe you can try and put some effort into making this year's posters for the fete. Last year's looked like they'd been drawn by a five-year-old.' Rita shot a final disapproving look at Mr Tim and then turned her back entirely. Breathing a sigh of relief, Mr Tim slipped back to his desk, nodding pointedly at the open door. Emmy grabbed my hand, but just as we made to sneak off down the aisle, a horrifying thought occurred to me – I hadn't been quick enough to close the pages we'd been looking at on the computer.

I whirled around just as Rita leaned in close to the screen, inspecting the pictures of Pride before her. I could only see her back, her slender shoulders rising and falling steadily, but I could imagine the sour look on her face as she took in people having fun, a concept I was sure she'd find unfamiliar.

'A load of rubbish,' she muttered to herself. Robin gave me a nudge and we slinked towards our freedom.

'Thanks, Mr Tim,' Emmy mouthed when we reached the door.

Mr Tim smiled and winked. 'Any time. Now, don't be strangers,' he said quietly.

We snuck outside, into the safety of the square, which was bustling in the sunlight as people prepared for the fete. If I'm being honest, they all looked thoroughly miserable. Jack the handyman was tackling a rather large arch of flowers, huffing and puffing and red in the face, while Miss Hart and Miss Finch directed him, equally as exhausted. Catherine had taken a short break in the door of the café, calling out encouragement as she mopped sweat from her brow.

'I think what we have is a good start,' Emmy said once we were a safe distance from the library. She dug out the notebook and started flicking through it. 'Figuring all this out is part of the fun, right?'

She had a spring in her step and a dreamy look in her eye. It was infectious and I started to conjure up visions of my own, images of a successful Pride day playing out in my mind, like the ones we'd just seen on the computer. As I imagined it, we were all there together, everyone in St Regent's Vale. Riley and Noah too, just as happy as anybody else.

'What do you say we head to the barn and start figuring out what we can do to get the ball rolling?' I said, suddenly eager to get the show on the road. Emmy and Robin didn't need much encouragement and raced off up the street.

I watched them go, pausing for just a moment. A swell of happiness, like a dash of sunshine, was starting to break through the clouds. I had friends who wanted to help me, and for the first time in a while, I felt like I was really *doing* something rather than just sitting back and waiting. It felt good to have something positive to focus on. Something that might just make a difference.

CHAPTER 20

A MEETING AT THE VILLAGE HALL

The next few days flew by in a flurry of planning, fuelled by countless pastries that Emmy kept baking and imaginations that were ready to run wild. However, it was way more difficult than any of us had expected. It wasn't like we didn't have ideas – we had plenty of those – but each one seemed too grand or too small, too out of reach or simply not good enough for what we had in mind.

It started out simple enough. Emmy said we needed balloons, and plenty of them, which we all agreed on. Robin added that we might need some banners and 'some of those rainbow flag things', which we also agreed on (although Emmy was still set on making her own following those eight easy steps). I threw in that we needed to sort out posters and invitations so people actually knew it was happening and would come along. Like I said, it was all perfectly doable.

And then Robin suggested we get a confetti cannon that we could stuff Riley into so that she could make a grand entrance, and things started to go rapidly downhill from there.

'What about horse rides?' Emmy asked, bouncing up and down on the spot as she added the idea to her notepad without a second thought.

'Well, I'm not so sure ...' I began, but Robin had already steamed ahead.

'Ooooh, and maybe we can order, like, an actual funfair? You know, like waltzers and stuff. It's a shame we probably can't have a rollercoaster set up that could go around the square and back again.'

'Do you think we can invite someone to sing? If we ask nicely, I think Little Mix would come. Do you think they charge a lot? How do we ask them? Do they have an email address?' Emmy bit the tip of her pen, staring dreamily off into space.

Robin and Emmy were so captivated by their ideas, they didn't even notice when I flopped down on to the floor with my head in my hands. This wasn't going to be as easy as I'd hoped. In fact, it was going to be nowhere near.

Since I was born with a mouth bigger than a cave and louder than a rocket launching to the moon, it's incredibly difficult for me to keep secrets. It's nearly impossible. Whenever I know a secret that I'm not allowed to tell, I can feel it bubbling away under my skin, ricocheting around my body like fireworks trying to find a way out into the open.

But although I was desperate to say something, I knew it was best to keep the idea a secret, at least for now. That meant whenever Mum asked why I looked so suspicious or what I'd been up to with Emmy and Robin, I would murmur something like, 'Oh, nothing, we just hung out and had some cakes.' I was sure she knew I was up to something else, but if she did, she chose to keep it to herself. This was probably because she still wouldn't tell us what she was up to out in Gran's shed. All we knew was that she kept disappearing out into the garden in her paint-spattered clothes, art supplies tucked under her arm.

You couldn't get much past Gran, though, who would

raise her eyebrows whenever she saw me walk through the door, flustered with guilt, narrowing her eyes as I tried to shuffle out of her sight.

'That one's up to something,' she'd muse to Mum when she thought I couldn't hear.

As for Noah, he'd taken to completely avoiding us altogether. Emmy and Robin wouldn't budge on telling me whatever secret they were keeping, which only made me like them more since they were being good friends to Noah, even when he wasn't around.

I thought I'd spotted Noah myself a couple of times, but even then, I couldn't be sure. I caught a glimpse of a diamond-patterned sweatshirt while waiting at the fish and chip shop, but it was gone when I did a double-take. Then I saw the flash of odd socks disappearing around a corner as I sat in Catherine's Café. But other than that, it seemed like Noah had barricaded himself in his house and was refusing to leave it in case he saw us and was pulled into our Pride hurricane.

'I just wish he'd talk to us,' I said for the hundredth time as we strolled towards the village square in the early afternoon sunshine. It had been another morning of planning, also known as another morning of trying to form ideas that weren't inviting world-famous girl bands or the swoon-worthy actor that Emmy had a crush on in one of her mum's favourite shows to Pride. For the millionth time, I wasn't being a fun sponge, I was just trying to be realistic!

'He'll come around when he's ready,' Emmy shrugged, seemingly unconcerned. 'He just needs some time.'

Robin was busy trying to race Smudge and Harry down the lane, so it was just the two of us and we walked in comfortable silence for a little longer.

'How are things with Riley?' Emmy asked gently. She had this way of pitching her voice just right, like she was letting you know that you could trust her to talk about things you might not want to talk about otherwise. And she always sounded like she really wanted to hear the answer too, not like she was asking just for the sake of something to talk about or because she was nosy.

'Better, but still not Riley,' I said with a sigh.

Now London Pride was done and dusted for another year, I was hopeful the old Riley would reappear. I'd been watching her even more closely after overhearing her conversation with Ziggy, trying to throw telepathic thoughts out into the air that she could talk to me if she wanted to. But she still seemed on edge – not so much sad or angry, but like she was living inside herself again and refusing to let any of us in. We only ever spoke properly just before bed, when I'd sometimes catch a glimpse of the old Riley. But even then, it was like we were skirting around the things we really wanted to say.

A bubble of chatter lingered over the square as we approached. People were huddled around the village hall steps, muttering to their neighbour restlessly. Every few seconds, a head would turn to look shiftily at the closed door, like something frightful might be hiding behind it.

'What's going on?' I asked as Emmy grabbed my hand and tugged me in the general direction of the village hall.

'It must be one of the meetings for the fete,' she murmured, peering around people to get a better view. 'It's basically just Rita bossing everybody around to make sure everything is perfect on the day. My parents will be there – I heard them whisking cakes past midnight in preparation for it.'

'It's the same old thing every summer,' I heard Porky mutter in front of us. He was trying to use his indoor voice with little success. 'This ruddy fete every darn year. I'm sick of it.'

The doors of the village hall suddenly burst open,

silencing the chatter. Rita stood at the top of the stairs, peering down at everybody like they were ants.

'Well, come in! We haven't got all day!' With a menacing look, she whirled around and stalked back into the shadows. Those by the steps tentatively followed, all in a jitter and sharing anxious looks.

'I wonder what . . .' Robin began saying, but the rest of his words were lost as I darted up the steps. I turned back and shrugged at the others, pointing inside. Emmy looked at me for a moment like I'd lost my mind, but Robin was already halfway to the stairs and Harry had scooped up Smudge to quickly follow, so she wasn't about to stay outside on her own.

'I just want to see what this is all about. Who knows, maybe we can get some ideas for Pride,' I said in a hushed whisper as Emmy slipped over to join us. 'We'll stay at the back, listen in, and leave before anybody even knows we're there.'

The village hall itself was simple and unnoteworthy – just a plain brick building that had probably seen better days. The smell was of something that had lived through a century or more and it clung around your nostrils when you breathed, thick and musty. Antique tables looked close to collapsing and the paint was beginning to flake in places. We crept towards a door that'd been left slightly ajar, the faded wooden floors squeaking under our feet.

'I'm glad you could all make it, even if *some* of you didn't manage to come to the last meeting.' Rita's drawl was really starting to grate on me.

We peeked inside to find a long, rectangular room, somehow even dustier than the foyer, with rows of chairs stretching towards the front. I fought the urge to sneeze as we crouched down at the back.

Rita sat at the front in a high-backed seat, legs crossed and a sour look twisting her face. Miss Hart and Miss Finch were huddled together, arms linked, shrinking into each other. Porky had forgotten to remove his butcher's hat and was spreading himself across three chairs. Doctor Dill sat rigid as a ruler in another seat, his thick glasses perched on the end of his nose.

'Now, with the summer fete only a fortnight away, this will be one of our final meetings to make sure your efforts aren't falling short of perfection. I'm sure you will miss our get-togethers to discuss such important matters –' Robin snorted at this – 'but alas, there is little time for sadness. I expect that you've all continued preparing to your *highest* standards to make sure it's a special day that will celebrate our marvellous village.'

'She means celebrate herself,' Emmy muttered.

Rita turned her eye on each of the faces before her. 'Miss Hart and Miss Finch, I don't think I need to tell you that your flower arrangements last year were flimsy at best. We may as well have used weeds for decoration instead. I assume you're working to fix that this year.'

Miss Hart and Miss Finch nodded quickly in unison.

'And Jack, I don't know how many times I have to tell you that the fences around the square need polishing,' Rita carried on. 'The walls are just *filthy* too. They won't do at all. Each brick must *gleam,* or we may as well hold our celebrations in a swamp.'

'I'll get right to it,' Jack said in a gruff and slightly grumpy voice.

'The Paceys?' Emmy and Harry tensed next to me. 'Ah yes, there you are. The cakes were almost stale last year, and there was far too much cream in the buns. I am all but shocked we didn't have diabetes come September.'

'She should make her own ruddy cakes,' Emmy huffed as her parents nodded up at the front, her sunshine for once completely dampened by Rita.

'Now, a reminder that there are to be no distractions of ANY kind in the lead-up to the fete,' Rita droned on. 'Every single person in this village should be making the most of their time to prepare. No excuse will be acceptable, and no other events will take priority. If you have birthdays or celebrations coming up, I suggest you find another weekend for them.'

I was stunned to see people nodding, as if Rita had simply requested that they pack sandwiches for a picnic. I glanced at Emmy and Robin, flabbergasted, but they just grimaced back with a knowing shrug.

And now I'd heard it for myself. There were to be no other events taking place that could disrupt Rita's precious weekend. That meant if we were going to do a Pride of our own, it definitely wouldn't have Rita's permission.

'Are there any questions?' Rita asked, already sounding bored of whatever other people had to say.

The few seconds of silence were broken by the booming sound of the village hall door being flung open. Every head in the room turned as the click-clack of heels peppered the foyer floor. Rita's eyes narrowed at the interruption, fury swimming in them. The footsteps got closer and closer until they were just outside the door. And then it opened.

There was a collective gasp, one that seemed to suck up all the air in the room, as a person so tall I thought he might touch the ceiling strode in. His height was helped by a pair of great platformed heels, the source of all the clicking and clacking, as well as a wig that was piled on top of his head like a spire. My jaw dropped as he strutted into the room, the light bouncing off his face, which had been painted with swirls of purple and blue. A drag queen in St Regent's Vale? Now that was something I hadn't expected to see. I immediately thought of Rue and Travis, who were always coming over and telling us about another drag show they'd been to recently and how we really should go to one ourselves. Now, it seemed like the show had come to us.

Rita looked for a moment as if she might faint at the sight of the stranger, but once she'd pulled herself together, her face clouded over. Her lips pursed and a glare shot up through her eyebrows. The stranger didn't falter once as people began to whisper behind their hands, eyes wide at the sight of him. When he reached the front of the room, he stood tall and fabulous, a beaming smile on his face.

'I thought I might find you here,' he said to Rita, his voice full and strong. 'Hi, Mum.'

CHAPTER 21

THE RETURN OF BUTTERCUP

The room was silent for the longest time, every pair of eyes fixed on Rita's son. Emmy looked just about ready to topple over, and Robin's mouth was open so wide that you could've parked a car in it. Smudge was the first to break the silence, yapping happily and trying to break free of Harry's arms to go over and greet this new person.

'I hope I'm not interrupting?'

His voice was loud enough that you could be mistaken for thinking he was actually speaking into a microphone hidden somewhere in his clothes. His lips had been painted a glossy red and were spread into a confident grin. I couldn't see any resemblance to Rita in his features, but then again, Rita wasn't wearing enough paint on her face to decorate a house with.

She did look furious, though. She was bristling with rage, struggling to contain it. Her entire body had gone rigid and she sat bolt upright, her mouth clamped into the thinnest and grimmest line. But her son just stood tall, one eyebrow raised slightly, waiting for someone else to speak.

'That's Norman,' Emmy whispered in my ear, a tremor of excitement wobbling her words. 'He lives in London. I don't know what he's doing here.' The name rang a vague bell, but I couldn't place why.

Finally, after what felt like an eternity, Rita stood up, fixing the room with an icy glare as if waiting for someone to challenge her. When she was met with nothing but silence, she stalked down the aisle without a word, storming past Norman and out through the doors, which slammed shut behind her.

Norman laughed to himself, unbothered. 'Maybe I should've sent a postcard instead.' He shrugged and turned to leave, waving to one old man sitting in the front row who looked like he'd seen an elephant doing a handstand. When Norman spotted the four of us and Smudge hiding behind the back row, he gave us a wink and another laugh before following in the footsteps of Rita. No sooner had the doors closed than excited whispers became animated gossip.

'I wonder why he's come back to the Vale?' Robin mused as we slipped back out into the square. It still felt like the whispers were following us, sweeping around the streets and through open doors. Sure enough, when I glanced around, huddles of people stood close together, looking over their shoulders the way people do when they're talking about things they shouldn't be. Rita and Norman might've been nowhere in sight, but their names were still skipping around the square all right.

Then the memory of walking into the village with Gran came back to me and I remembered where I'd heard that name before. 'He's back to help clear out Wendy's house,' I said, reciting what Jack had told us outside her cottage when we first arrived.

Emmy mulled it over, nodding to herself. 'Makes sense, I guess. I heard my parents talking about Wendy after the funeral, and how Norman would've happily swapped Rita for her. They were talking to our neighbours over the fence, and they said Norman and Rita never really got on when he was a teenager, so he used to spend all his time at Wendy's house instead. Then he moved to London and stopped coming back home at all.'

'To be fair, I wouldn't come back home if Rita was my mum either,' Robin murmured, and Harry nodded quickly in agreement.

'Why didn't they get on?' I asked as we moved through the square and started off towards the Den. There was still a lot of planning to do if our Secret Sunshine Project was going to get off the ground at all. I had a sneaking suspicion Emmy was a handful of ideas away from asking about the possibility of unicorns.

'Well, you saw him back there, didn't you? Rita has never liked anybody who stands out. She likes everything to be plain and boring, and for everyone to know their place and stay in it. Norman's the complete opposite of that. If it were up to Rita, only girls would wear makeup and wigs and dresses, and boys would just be . . . I don't know, all muddy and gross from crawling around in fields all day.' Emmy looked glum and miserable for a moment, but she quickly brightened up, grabbing my arm and pulling me into a skip.

'But that's what's so great about Norman. I've only met him once, when he came back for the funeral, but everybody said he was the nicest person they'd ever met. So what if he wears makeup? It's just colour on your face, isn't it? It's like face paint.'

'Ziggy wears makeup,' Robin said, and Emmy grinned so wide her face could barely contain it.

'He wears it better than Mum – even she admits it!'

We'd just passed the church, leaving the afternoon bustle behind us as everybody frantically got back to work on their fete preparations, when a voice shouted out my name. Confused, because it definitely didn't belong to Mum, Gran or Riley, I turned to find Noah running towards us, flustered and breathing heavily.

'What's up, No?' Robin said as he caught up to us. He looked both concerned and a little relieved to see Noah out of the house and actually talking to us, a feeling we could all relate to.

Noah stopped a few paces away, looking nervous and embarrassed. He caught my eye and I tried to smile encouragingly but he quickly glanced back down at the ground, his hands dug deep into the pockets of his orange shorts.

'Can I talk to you?' he mumbled.

'Of *course* you can talk to us, silly,' Emmy said gently,

stepping into the space between us and throwing a comforting arm around Noah. He relaxed a little, but he still appeared nervous.

'I mean, can I talk to you, Bea? Just quickly – I promise it won't take long.' Robin and Emmy didn't seem fazed and instead nodded so quickly in my direction that I nearly shouted 'YES' in response. Noah mooched over to one side of the lane, while Robin, Emmy, Harry and Smudge started wandering off up the road.

Noah didn't seem to know where to start, so I jumped in first to save him. 'How's it going?' I asked, casually enough because I still didn't know what all of this was about. 'Is everything okay? We've missed you.'

Noah took a deep breath, still looking anywhere but at me and biting down on his lip while he collected up all the words he wanted to say. 'I . . . well, I wanted to say I'm sorry,' he mumbled. 'You know, for kinda disappearing when you had your idea.' He rocked back on his heels, shuffling around on the spot some more. 'It's just . . . well, I was a little scared, and not just because of Rita. I don't know if Emmy and Robin told you anything . . .'

He trailed off, letting his words hang in the warm air around us, buzzing like insects out in the fields.

'I think I've always felt a little different. Like, I don't fit in here or there or anywhere else. I've been thinking about it for a while, since before you even arrived, but then when you told us about Riley and this London Pride thing, it started to make more sense.'

I remembered sitting in the computer chair after Noah and finding the pictures of London Pride already loaded on the screen, and how Emmy and Robin hadn't seemed surprised. They didn't want to say anything because it wasn't their place. The missing pieces of the picture in my head were starting to come together.

'I wanted to help with the Pride thing, but I didn't want to ... I don't know. I didn't want to speak about it yet because I wasn't sure if I understood it, and I still don't know if I do.' Noah finally looked at me properly. He was nervous, but behind the fear, there was something else – something that wasn't scared. It was more like relief, like he'd been holding on to a breath that he was now ready to let go of.

'I just think Pride might mean the same to me as it does to Riley, and to all those other people around the world who might be like me. I was scared to admit that in case it changed things. I didn't know what my grandma would say, or what other people would think. But seeing how you guys talk about it as if it's not a big deal made me feel like maybe it doesn't have to change things. And I don't know if you still want me to help, but if you'll have me back ...'

I couldn't even try to fight the smile on my face. Before he could say another word, I leaped forward and wrapped my arms around Noah, hugging him tight and hooting and hollering without a care in the world about who could hear. A few seconds later, I heard the others racing towards us, laughing as they threw their arms around us too. And there we were, in the middle of the road, looking like a bunch of crazy kids who couldn't stop laughing and whooping and hugging each other silly.

When we finally broke apart, I felt more confident than ever that we were going to make something great. Not just for Riley, not just for Noah, but for everyone in St Regent's Vale who might need it.

I thrust my hand into the middle of us all, daring the others to join me. Emmy put her hand on mine first, quickly followed by Robin. Noah put his hand on top, and Harry scooted into the circle to add his hand and Smudge's paw to the pile.

'What do you say we go and plan a Pride this village

will never forget?' I grinned, but before the others could say a word, another voice behind me beat them to the punch.

'I couldn't think of a better idea.'

CHAPTER 22

YOU CAN CALL ME NORMAN

We all spun around in a tizzy, terrified that our idea had been rumbled before we'd even planned it out properly. When I saw who it was, I just stood there like a dummy, mouth agape, staring up at the tallest man I'd ever seen.

Norman peered down at us all inquisitively, somehow even taller than he'd seemed before. A smirk was tugging up one side of his mouth as his eyes roamed over each of us in turn. They lit up completely when they landed on Smudge, who fought his way out of Harry's arms and over to Norman's feet, where he licked at his ankles and shins.

'What a GORGEOUS little angel,' Norman sang, bending down to scoop him up and get a better look at him. Smudge barked and wagged his tail in mid-air, now trying to lick Norman's nose. He pulled him in close for a hug, then popped him down on the floor and took us all in once more. 'Now, what's this I hear about Pride?'

Emmy, Robin, Noah and Harry all looked at me, stepping back slightly to let me have centre stage. I didn't know what to say or where to start, or even if I should trust Norman with our secret plan that, if we were being honest, still needed a lot of work. But something about Norman, his loud but friendly voice, his curious eyes, and the swirls of colours that made up his face, made me relax. Besides, we could definitely do with some help.

'Well, it was just a silly idea really,' I started, shifting on the spot under Norman's watchful stare.

'A great idea!' Emmy chirped up, lending her support. Robin, Noah and Harry all nodded fiercely, and I felt a surge of encouragement rear its head and put weight behind my words.

'So, it all began when we moved away from London for the summer,' I started again, standing up a little taller. I explained about Riley, how we'd had to miss out on London Pride. 'I just thought it'd be great to have something like Pride here. Something that Riley and Ziggy and everyone else in the village can enjoy for a day.'

Norman's expression had become more serious, the

playful twinkle in his eye almost gone completely. He looked like he was mulling something over or deciding if we were in trouble. By the time I'd finished, I wasn't sure if telling Norman was the best idea after all. I stepped back into line with the others, almost expecting Norman to completely shut the whole thing down. And what would we do if he *did* think it was terrible?

But eventually, he smiled. It was small and thoughtful, like the smiles Mum used to give to Dad just before she'd tell him how much she loved him, or how much she loved us. I relaxed a little, and felt the others do the same beside me.

'That's quite possibly the best idea I've ever heard in my life,' Norman said, shaking his head with a hearty laugh. 'Genius! It's about time someone tried to spruce this place up with a bit of sparkle, I can tell you that much!' Norman held his hand out to us with a beaming grin. 'Buttercup,' he said proudly, and I frowned because nobody had told me that was his name. I tried to cover up the frown, but Norman/Buttercup saw it and burst out laughing all over again.

'You can call me Norman, though. Buttercup's just for when I'm on stage or got one of these silly things on.' He pointed to the wig sitting on his head like a lick of ice cream.

'I don't think it's silly at all,' Emmy said, in awe now that she was able to inspect it properly without looking rude. 'It's so beautiful!'

Norman spread his arms wide and hooted another laugh. 'You'll go far with compliments like that, young lady,' he barked. 'I do admit, it's one of my best. I wanted to make sure I gave my mother an awful fright when I turned up. She's lucky my friend Lester talked me out of arriving in a wedding dress – I do the best Princess Diana in east London, veil and all!'

My mind boggled at the thought of Norman showing up to the village hall meeting in a wedding dress. I would've paid to see Rita's reaction to that.

'Anyway, this Pride you want to throw. Any ideas on how you want to do it yet?' Norman looked at us expectantly, eagerly awaiting our grand plans. Except, of course, there weren't any that didn't include Little Mix or confetti cannons.

'Well . . .' I shrugged with a blush, but Norman waved off my shame with a flick of his hand.

'No worries at all. You little lot pop over tomorrow once

I'm settled and we'll brainstorm it together. I'm staying over at Dawnlight Cottage, where dear old Wendy used to live. God knows I wouldn't stay at that devil's lair I'm meant to call home. The memories I have of that place – it's enough to make one shudder!' Norman acted out a dramatic shiver and a wave of giggles rippled through us. Before he turned to go, Norman stopped, narrowing his eyes in Emmy's direction.

'That red hair reminds me of Mrs Pacey-Jones . . .' he said, and Emmy nodded brightly. 'In that case, if you could sneak over some of her wonderful cream buns, you'd be an angel sent from heaven!'

With a wave, Norman headed off towards Wendy's cottage, leaving us to stand around and wonder what had just happened. I didn't want to get ahead of myself, but it seemed like our Pride might be starting to pick up some steam after all. The thought was enough to make me giddy and lightheaded. If we had Norman on our side, we'd be pretty much unstoppable.

After the day we'd had, I felt like nothing could ruin my good mood. I'd been teetering on the edge of it for a while, especially since making new friends in St Regent's Vale, but now the colours were beginning to emerge from behind that grey cloud. Things were definitely looking up.

But when I got home later that evening, there was a sombre mood lying over everything like a blanket. It was quiet, which was the first sign that something was wrong, with no game show or news channel blaring from the TV in the living room. In fact, the living room was entirely empty. Mum and Gran were in the kitchen, hunched over the dining table, their hands entwined over the wood. They'd clearly been discussing something serious but stopped when I appeared in the doorway.

'What's up?' I asked suspiciously, looking from one face to the other. Mum gave me a wobbly smile and cleared her throat, letting go of Gran's hand to lean back in her chair and sigh.

'We're just having a chat, honey. About ... well, you know, everything.' Mum looked down at the table, lowering her voice as if it might scare me away. 'It's going to be the anniversary next weekend.'

I felt my face fall and at the same time my whole body went light, like I might be able to drift up and touch the ceiling, or just float straight through it and keep on going towards the sky. I'd let the idea of Pride take up as much space in my head as it could so I wouldn't have to think about it. But, of course, the thought of Dad and the anniversary had been blooming in my mind, stretching its tentacles further through my body until it had settled in every part of me. The only reason the overwhelming sadness hadn't consumed me entirely was because Pride was shining a light in the darkness, keeping me afloat.

'We'll all be fine,' Gran said. A determination had crept into her eyes, which were slightly red from tearing up. 'We're allowed to be sad, to cry and be angry. We have to let ourselves feel however our bodies want to feel. But we must also let ourselves be free to feel the good things too – to remember your dad and to smile and laugh at the memories we still hold close to us.'

Gran raised her eyebrows and nodded over my shoulder, and I suddenly felt a presence behind me. Riley stepped out of the shadows of the hallway, her own eyes glassy and sparkling with tears. Her bottom lip trembled but she didn't turn and flee. Instead, she rested a hand on my shoulder and stood her ground. Mum and Gran both smiled at the sight of us standing together, although Mum looked as if she were about to burst into tears all over again.

'This family has been through a lot in the past year,' Gran carried on. 'We've all lost somebody close to us who we loved, and still love now. But together, as a family, we can help to hold each other up, okay? We don't need to go through this grief – through any of our feelings – alone when we have each other.' Gran grasped Mum's hand and cradled it in her own. Mum wasn't even trying to stop herself from crying now, and neither was Riley. I was doing my best to keep it in, scared that if I let myself go, I wouldn't be able to put the pieces back together again. Fortunately, Gran took it upon herself to lighten the mood.

'Now, the first thing we can do to hold each other up is get over here and help me out of this bloody chair!' We all burst out laughing, coming together to put our hands around Gran and prop her up into a standing position. 'Whose idea was it to get chairs harder than concrete?' she muttered, rubbing circles into her back and hobbling off for the kettle. 'It'll be lucky if any of us have spines left by next week.'

We spent the night watching terrible game shows that Gran chose as she was in charge of the remote control, because some things never change. But nobody complained or grumbled or moaned. We all settled in and laughed along, shouting out answers at the screen and whooping with delight when we got one right. Not that anybody was keeping score, but Gran definitely won.

It felt like I had my family back together again. Like we had my sister back again too, which made me want to laugh and cry all at the same time. There was a glaring space where Dad should've been, but it no longer felt like a cold and empty void between us. If anything, it now felt like a warm light, wrapping itself around us. It felt like Dad was still here.

CHAPTER 23

A SUPERHERO WEARS A DISGUISE

For the first time since we arrived in St Regent's Vale, I woke up the next morning to the gentle patter of rain. I clambered out of bed, nearly tripping over my sheets and faceplanting the floor, to leap up on to the sleeping lump that was Riley before whipping open the curtains. She groaned, disappearing under the duvet and muttering something about it being the middle of the night.

Sure enough, the sky was a steely grey without a patch of blue in sight. Everything outside was soaking wet and glum, a relentless drizzle coating everything. I just hoped it wasn't an omen for how things would go when we went to see Norman.

I wasn't sure if I needed to prepare anything before going to Dawnlight Cottage and, if I was being honest, I felt nervous all over again. The Pride idea had been mine after all, and although the others were almost as keen to make it happen too, if it all went wrong or didn't work out, it was pretty much down to me, and that scared me more than anything. Sure, it'd be embarrassing, but there'd also be this crushing defeat, like I'd let everybody down, and I couldn't bear the thought of that. The biggest part of me wanted to do this for Riley, for Ziggy, and for Noah too. But another, smaller, part of me wanted to impress Norman and not just look like a kid who'd been dreaming way too much.

'What's got your tongue?' Gran asked at the kitchen table, shuffling her newspaper around to get a better look at me. 'You're usually chewing up my ear about something or other. What is it?'

I tried to shrug it off nonchalantly, but Gran just narrowed her eyes, raking them over me like she could X-ray my head and see all of my thoughts.

'Just sleepy,' I said, throwing in a fake yawn for good measure. Gran pursed her lips but was interrupted by Mum charging into the kitchen with her painting supplies under her arm.

'I'm off out to the shed,' she announced, heading for

the back door. She'd changed into her painting overshirt, which had smears of colour all over it, and a pair of jeans that had seen more paint than the walls of an average house.

'What *is* she up to out there?' Gran murmured, peeking over her newspaper suspiciously.

I shrugged. 'It's a secret, apparently.'

Gran went back to her paper, muttering, 'As long as she's not painting in here and redecorating my carpets.'

With Mum out of the way and Gran occupied with a crossword, I dashed back upstairs, got washed and dressed and was out of the front door with a small umbrella in record time, running in the direction of Wendy's cottage. Emmy, Robin, Noah, Harry and Smudge were already waiting, huddled closely together in various coloured rain jackets. Emmy carried a hamper in the crook of her arm and the smell of cakes and pastries wafted up to greet me as I skidded to a stop outside the gate, my stomach grumbling so loudly that I mumbled an apology. In my rush to join the others, I'd forgotten to grab some breakfast.

'This is SO exciting!' Emmy squealed, nearly yanking my arm out of its socket as she dragged me up the path to the front door. The garden was now just as neat and tidy as the rest of the cottages on the lane after Jack had attacked it with the lawnmower, and flowers were blooming in patches around the edges. The rain had muddied up parts of the grass, but there was something picturesque about it anyway.

'BUTTERCUP!' Harry yelled as he tore between us to get to the front door first, Smudge hot on his heels and barking for Norman too. Robin tripped and nearly fell into the wheelie bin in his excitement to follow, and Noah looked just about ready to burst. It was Emmy who raised her hand to knock, but before she could, the door flew open and there was Norman.

He looked very different to the day before, when he'd been dressed and painted in every colour of the rainbow. Now he stood at the front door with a fresh and clean face, short hair that was mostly grey and clothes that wouldn't have looked out of place on any of the people in the village square on a regular Monday morning.

Norman laughed at the look on our faces, holding his stomach as he bent double and began spluttering. 'I'm not a sight for sore eyes this morning, I'll give you that!' He chuckled, standing aside to let us in out of the rain.

'I don't wake up looking like the glamorous movie starlet you were expecting, you know!'

After pouring us all steaming mugs of hot chocolate, Norman herded us into the living room, where a bunch of sofas and armchairs in all different colours and materials took up most of the space. Norman settled into a blue velvet chair, while Emmy and Harry scooted up into a dark leather one. Noah and Robin shared a sofa that was the funniest shade of orange, and I took up a spot next to Smudge on a bejewelled pouffe.

'Quite the character, wasn't she?' Norman said, gesturing at the room. There were shelves and bookcases everywhere, each surface cluttered with various ornaments and trinkets. Gilded mirrors and eccentric pictures hung from the walls, which had been painted in swatches of colour that reminded me of Mum's painting palettes. Even the shade covering the big light was something special, a pattern of multicoloured elephants forming a train around the brim.

'I think that's why she liked me so much,' Norman mused. 'I always used to tell old Wendy that she might've been a drag queen in another life. Or maybe a tarot card reader, what with all the crystal balls she had stuffed into every corner of the house.' Norman sighed, smiling to himself. His eyes had a faraway look, no doubt picturing a time when he was back with Wendy. But after a moment, he dragged himself out of it and beamed at us instead. 'She'd love this idea of yours, I can tell you that much!'

'It was all Bea's idea!' Emmy said brightly, pointing at me like Norman might have forgotten who I was. 'And it's brilliant! We saw all the pictures of Pride and I just know it's going to be great if we can make one of our own!'

I shuffled on my pouffe, the beads jingling together. 'I'm just ... I'm not sure how you actually do it. Make your own Pride, I mean.' I shrugged and tried not to look embarrassed, but Norman waved me off in a way that made me smile.

'Nonsense! You don't need all that much at all. All you need is the *want* to do it. Have you got that?' We all nodded, and Norman raised his eyebrows with a single nod as if the case was closed.

'Well, there we go! That's how we start! These Prides you see around the world – yes, they're mostly huge and expensive, but it was never about that in the beginning. Pride was about standing up for what you believe in. It was about standing up for the rights of everybody, no matter who they are and who they love. Pride was about protesting and sticking it to the man and saying, "We've had enough of the way you treat our community, and we won't take it any more!"'

Norman leaped up, a hand over his chest like he was reciting a national anthem. Robin whooped and clapped, which only egged him on more. 'You need nothing more than the want to say something – the *need* to say something. And you don't need money or sponsorships or fancy outfits to say it, to *feel* it. You just need *you*.'

Norman suddenly bolted from the living room and high-tailed it up the stairs, calling for us to follow. We all shared a confused look, but curiosity got the better of us and we scrambled after him. We fell into a small room that had maybe once been a bedroom but was now a study, with an ancient computer sitting between two over-stuffed bookcases. Norman was already in the computer chair, firing up the internet and opening a social media page in a new tab. He leaned in close, typing in a password for a profile that had his name attached, before dragging the mouse around the screen and pulling up a photo album.

After a few clicks, Norman found the picture he was

looking for, hooting to himself and slapping his thigh. 'Now, didn't I look a penny short of a pound back then!'

A much younger Norman, maybe eighteen or so, stood in the middle of the road, a crowd of people behind him. He wore tattered jeans with rips up both legs, and a flimsy white vest that was so stained it looked grey. He stood defiantly, hands in the air and holding one side of a ripped cardboard box, on which was written: 'OUR RIGHTS ARE HUMAN RIGHTS!' The hair alone, which was curly on top and long at the back, was enough to tell me that this picture had been taken a long time ago.

'The 1990s, up in Manchester I think,' Norman said proudly. I gawped at a decade I could barely conceive, one that had passed way before I was even born. 'We were a right little band of vagabonds, up and down the country protesting wherever we could.'

The next picture was a close-up of Norman, looking directly into the camera with a steely look in his eyes. They were country-grass-green, full of life and fire. Even though he wasn't dressed up in his Buttercup clothes, his eyelids still had licks of colour on them, pulled up to his hairline in dramatic flicks.

'Why do you wear makeup?' Noah asked. For a

moment, I thought he might reach out and touch the screen. Then he seemed to realize he'd spoken out loud and immediately flushed a furious shade of crimson, stuttering an apology. Norman just laughed and leaned back in his chair thoughtfully. Before he spoke, he seemed to come up with an idea, hopping up and diving into the bedroom. He came back with a big bag, stuffed with brushes still tinged with the blush of colours they'd been dipped in. Norman unzipped the bag completely as we all gathered around in a semi-circle to look at the contents.

'Have you worn makeup before?' Norman asked, the end of one brush between his teeth. Noah shook his head, seemingly dazed and a little terrified of a dusty pot Norman was opening. 'How about we give it a try now? This is a safe space, just between us.' Noah looked like he might faint, but Emmy put a comforting hand on his shoulder and he seemed to relax, nodding quickly before he could change his mind.

'Eyes closed then, young man, and I'll tell you a story as we go,' Norman started, dipping the brush into the pot and sweeping it across Noah's eyelid. 'Now, when I was a boy, I was all nervous and shy and could never speak up in front of people. I know you might find it hard to believe now that I'm this fabulous monster, but it's true. I barely said boo to a goose until I was a teenager.'

We watched eagerly as Norman opened up an eyeshadow palette and browsed the options intently. He hovered over a deep red, then shook his head and thoughtfully assessed the greens. Finally, he grinned and went for a summer-sky-blue, the kind that had been swallowed up by the clouds today.

'But when I got to university, I met my family. Not my *family* family,' he added quickly, 'but my friends, the ones I chose to be my family. I'd never had friends like it, coming from a small place like this, and for the first time ever, I felt like I wasn't the only person living outside this small box that the world tells us we should stay in. I finally had friends who loved and accepted who I was, and I loved every single second. There's no greater feeling in this world than someone seeing the real you and not only accepting you, but loving you too.'

Norman assessed the blue on Noah's eyelids, which was already making me a little giddy with excitement, and dived into a pink that was almost purple. Emmy could barely contain herself – she was practically vibrating on the spot. Harry was leaning in so close to Noah that

Norman flicked the brush in his direction and grazed a dash of pink on his cheek, which Harry thought was hilarious. Even Robin, who'd looked nothing less than suspicious at the start, was inspecting the scene with an eager anticipation.

'Now, when I discovered makeup, I thought it was just for girls and something I shouldn't touch. But one night, when we were all a little too merry, one of the girls I lived with asked to borrow my face for a beauty assignment and I agreed. I couldn't blame her for asking!' Norman framed his face with his hands like he was a picture, or a goddess looking up at the sun. 'And when I saw myself staring back in the mirror, all dolled up, I nearly fell off the stool. I looked GORGEOUS, of course, but I didn't recognize myself sitting there. I felt different. Powerful even – like I was a whole other person.'

Norman leaned in close and carefully brushed the final strokes on to Noah's eyelids in deep concentration. The brief silence was unbearable, and I could tell Noah was fighting not to tear open his eyes and see what was going on.

'Of course, the makeup itself doesn't change who you are. Not really, anyway. I'm still the same person, whether

I have it on my face or not. But ...' Norman nodded with satisfaction and guided Noah, eyes still closed, over to the mirror. 'It's my armour, and when I wear it, I feel like nothing or nobody could ever hurt me. When I'm all dressed up as Buttercup, it's like this whole other person climbs out of me. And that person *is* me, but unafraid, unfiltered and unflinchingly themselves. Buttercup reminds me that I have this power inside of me to be any person I want to be. And that's how we should all feel.'

Tapping Noah on the shoulder, Norman stepped back with a flourish. Noah took a deep breath and slowly opened one eye, then the other, peeking at his reflection in the mirror. When he caught sight of himself, his mouth dropped open with a gasp, his eyes widening. The rest of us gasped too as we got a proper look, Emmy nearly exploding through the roof next to me.

'How do you feel?' Norman asked, grinning behind Noah in the mirror.

Noah leaned in close, so he was centimetres away from his reflection. He was silent for a moment, taking it all in. Then he leaned back with a smile.

'I feel like a superhero,' he said. 'I feel invincible.'

CHAPTER 24

THE NOT-SO-SECRET-
ANY-MORE PROJECT

By the time we left Wendy's cottage, Emmy's notebook was brimming with new ideas, adding a kind of sunshine to the day. Norman had been patient, sitting back and letting us take the lead on what we wanted to do and how we wanted to do it, only interrupting to offer help if we got stuck.

There were a lot of things we needed, and we still had to figure out how to get some of them, but the list looked a little something like this:

1. Balloons – lots and lots of balloons
2. Flags and banners
3. A stage for people to stand and speak on

4. Market stalls, because the people of St Regent's Vale love those
5. Music and speakers (and Norman said we needed a microphone too)
6. Invites and posters – you know, so people would actually know the whole thing was happening.

'Where do you even get a stage from?' I'd grumbled when Robin had that idea. Norman said it was important for people to be able to speak and maybe to also have performances of some kind. But getting an entire stage seemed like one of the more impossible tasks we had on the list.

'Well, you don't *need* a stage,' Norman had said. 'You just need something that's stage-like. The village hall steps, for example. They're higher up and look down over the square – if you dress them up with Pride decorations, that could be your stage. No purchase needed.'

'This is why we needed an adult involved,' Robin murmured, crossing out the stage invention he'd been sketching.

The only point that nobody could seem to agree on was when St Regent's Vale Pride should take place. I was the only person with a specific date in mind – I'd been thinking about it for a few days already – and I didn't want to budge from it: August the sixth.

'That's only a week away!' Noah chirped, fluttering his hand against his leg. 'And besides, it'd be impossible to do it then anyway.'

'That's the weekend before Rita's fete,' Emmy explained, sighing softly.

'She'll never let anything overshadow it,' Robin added, and everybody except Norman and Smudge nodded.

'Maybe it can be a few weeks later? That'll give us more time to get organized,' Emmy tried, but I shook my head.

'It has to be August the sixth,' I said quietly, staring at the carpet to avoid the eyes I knew were on me. My cheeks were getting hot, and I clasped my hands together to stop them from shaking. The date was more important to me than anything, one that was now tattooed in my memory, like birthdays and Christmas. It had to be then.

But I'd been keeping the reason away from the others, hiding it behind that wall of mine, refusing to let anybody look past it. Noah had trusted me with his secret, and the others had stood with me as we planned a Pride that was sure to rattle Rita. They'd let me into their group like it was the easiest thing in the world. Now, I had to trust them.

'It's my dad's anniversary,' I murmured, so faintly that the others had to lean in to hear me properly. 'He died last year. That's . . . that's why Riley's been so sad. Pride meant a lot to her because it was the last place we went together as a family. It means a lot to us all.'

With each word, I removed another brick from my wall, revealing the feelings that I'd been ignoring since Dad had gone. But although I could feel the grief swelling up inside me, I could feel something else too – relief as I set free what I'd been hiding.

'This whole year has been miserable. It's like the sun's gone behind a cloud and hasn't come back out from the other side yet. But it's starting to. I can feel it.' Now that I'd taken my wall down, I started to cry and I didn't even try to stop because these were my friends and what shame was there in tears? 'We'll never be able to go back to that place, when Dad was still here, but maybe there's another place, where things are different but might still be okay after all.'

Emmy didn't waste a second in coming to sit beside me.

She cupped my hand in hers, giving it a gentle squeeze. 'I think you're really brave,' she said quietly, tears of her own sparkling in her eyes. I sniffed, squeezing her hand back, saying thank you in a way that didn't need words. Harry scooped up Smudge and popped him in my lap which, I must admit, did make me feel better.

'It has to be that date,' I said, scratching Smudge behind the ears. 'I know it might be selfish, but it just makes sense. August the sixth means so much to us. It'd be the perfect way to do this.'

Noah and Robin still looked a little nervous, but it was Emmy who leaned forward with a determined nod of her head. 'August the sixth it is.' Noah and Robin, after a moment, agreed too.

One of the biggest questions still remained, though – how were we going to announce the whole thing? We were already close to the big date, just a single week away, and with so little time to spare, we had to get the word out and around St Regent's Vale immediately. But there was one big obstacle in our way, and she would be furious when she found out – Rita.

'Norman didn't seem too bothered about Rita finding out, so why should we be?' Emmy said as we left

Dawnlight Cottage and headed in the direction of the shops to buy snacks for the barn.

'Well, that's because he's *Buttercup.*' Noah sighed, pulling on his cuffs and looking up and down the street as if Rita might appear at any moment. Even though he'd wiped off the eyeshadow, smudges of pink and blue remained. 'Buttercup isn't scared of anybody. We're just five kids and a dog.'

'Hey!' me and Emmy said together, offended. 'Just because we're kids doesn't mean we can't make a difference, does it?' Emmy added. Noah looked allergic to the idea, the superhero with blue and pink eyeshadow long gone.

We could see preparations for the fete happening all around us. As we walked, we saw Doctor Dill grumpily mowing his front garden, flinging the lawnmower this way and that like he'd rather be doing anything else in the world. In the square, Jack was polishing the railings, muttering a few choice words I'm sure we weren't supposed to hear under his breath. Catherine was making jams in the café, her apron smeared with splodges that hadn't made it into jars. As the rain picked up, we ducked under a tree by the church, peering out through the drizzle as the people of St Regent's Vale hurried by. Something as measly as rain wasn't going to stop them from preparing for the fete – not when Rita's wrath was at stake.

'Let's focus on something that's not so scary for now.' Emmy flipped open her notepad and reread her hastily scrawled notes, which somehow still seemed to be neater than my best handwriting. 'Norman said he'd take care of finding our floats for the day, and he also said he'd invite some special guests. So all we really have to focus on is . . .'

Emmy paused and closed the notebook quietly. Noah raised his eyebrows, smug. 'Telling everybody, including Rita.' Emmy stuck out her tongue, unzipping her bag to put our plans safely back inside, but it slipped out of her hand and landed in a muddy puddle. She gasped, not at her now soaking notepad, but at an official-looking wellington boot that had appeared right beside it.

'And what's *this*?' Rita snapped at us, and we all jumped back in fright. We hadn't even heard her coming. Dozer growled by her side, straining against his leash. Robin backed away and nearly toppled over the low church wall, Noah saving him by grabbing his jacket at the last second. 'Don't you have better things to do than to stand around causing trouble?'

The others squirmed backwards some more, but I was tired of being scared. Even though my heart was almost in my mouth – beating through my entire body – I didn't want to back down this time.

'We're not causing any trouble,' I said, my words stronger than I'd expected them to be. My voice was a notch higher than usual, but Rita didn't seem to notice, zeroing in on me with disdain, her eyes narrowing until they were snake-like slits. I tried to stand up a little straighter, refusing to wilt. Maybe it was the attitude of my great-grandad that everybody told me I had that spurred me on. 'We're just standing under a tree, out of the rain so we don't get wet.'

Rita's face flushed with fury, her spectacles almost vibrating off her nose. She bunched her hands into fists, gritting her teeth and breathing heavily, just like Dozer.

'How *dare* you answer me back?' she spat, bearing down on me like I was something for her to eat. I tried to stand my ground, but I took a small step back, more to get away from her hot breath than anything else. But she smelled blood and a manic glint flashed in her eye. 'This is *my* village. Everything and everyone in it belongs to me. You and your smart mouth would do well to remember that.

I can make life *very* difficult for you and your family so long as they live under my watch.'

I glared up at Rita, folding my arms and holding myself firm so my feet wouldn't betray me. 'My gran would love to see you try.'

'Your gran will not protect you in this village. I don't care who she is.' Rita took one step more. 'I'm warning you, little girl – watch what you do or say next. I have a very good memory, and I hold an even longer grudge.'

'If I were you, I'd leave my little sister alone.'

Rita whirled around, set to explode, and found Riley and Ziggy standing there, soaking wet. Ziggy looked fearful but stood loyally by Riley's side all the same. Riley, on the other hand, was glowering at Rita, her arms also folded across her chest. I'd never seen her look more furious in my whole entire life.

'Bullying kids? That's what you do to pass the time?'

Rita's eyes flashed down to Riley's rainbow badge, pinned to her jacket, and it seemed to infuriate her more. She pulled herself up to her full height but Riley didn't waver.

'I'll be watching each and every one of you,' Rita said menacingly.

Riley snorted. 'It sounds like you need a hobby then.' She nodded to me. 'Come on, you lot. Let's leave her to people-watch in peace.'

We didn't need to be told twice, clambering over each other to skirt around Rita. She was so angry I thought she might take off into the sky, but Riley just started walking off up the street, the rest of us on her tail. We weren't even at the corner yet, though, when Emmy stopped dead in her tracks.

'My notebook!'

We all spun around to where we'd been stood, but we were too late. With a curled lip, Rita bent down, scooped it up, and inspected the cover. With one final scowl, she stalked off in the opposite direction, our secret sunshine project clutched in her hands.

CHAPTER 25

IT'S TIME TO TELL

We couldn't help but look over our shoulders after that, like Rita was coming to get us and we were just sitting ducks, waiting to be caught. We avoided every place we thought she might be and stayed out of the village square at all costs. We didn't even go back to the Den, terrified that now Rita had our notebook, she'd know all our secrets and would be lying in wait, ready to pounce.

But that didn't stop our planning. We'd lost the notebook, but we weren't going to let that stand in our way. With time running out, we turned our efforts up a gear and started putting together the best possible Pride we could.

Dawnlight Cottage was our headquarters, and Norman was our mentor. I knew he could organize this whole thing in his sleep, but I wanted to prove that we could do it – that *I* could do it. We sat on the floor of Wendy's living room the following day surrounded by loose bits of paper that had been scrawled and sketched upon until there was no blank space left. We had lists and diagrams scattered everywhere, along with scissors and Sellotape and Blu Tack to pin things up on the walls. It was like a colour bomb had gone off in Wendy's house and left a rainbow of chaos in its wake.

As for Rita, even when we couldn't see her, it felt like danger hovered just out of sight. We were waiting for something bad to happen. And, of course, Rita didn't let us down.

'SHE'S MOVED THE FETE TO AUGUST THE SIXTH?! But that's our day!' I yelped. My eyes felt like they were bulging out of my head as I read the paper that had been pinned to the noticeboard outside the village hall. We'd had to chance a trip through the square in order to get to the post office.

'She's read the notebook,' Noah said, taking a step closer to Robin as if Rita might leap out at any moment and rip our heads off. 'She knows about Pride. This is her way of making a threat.'

Emmy shook her head in disbelief, stepping up to the noticeboard to get a better look. 'The annual summer fete will now take place on August the sixth. Attendance is highly recommended,' she read aloud. 'She can't do that!'

'Who's going to stop her?' Robin said with a defeated shrug.

Norman laughed it off with a wave of his hand. 'A little piece of paper's not going to ruin our big day. If she wants war, then I'm *more* than happy to go to battle.' He yanked the notice down, scrunched it up into a ball and threw it into a nearby bin. 'Now, where are we on those posters?'

Preparing our posters meant standing in line at the post office to use the printer, so we'd have them ready to hang up in the square. Mrs Winchester, who sat behind the counter with a bow in her hair and enjoyed nothing more than knowing other people's business, watched us suspiciously as Robin tried to stand in the way, shielding the posters from sight.

'Do you need any help?' Mrs Winchester asked sweetly, already clambering out of her chair to try and get a better glimpse at what we were up to.

'No, thanks, Mrs Winchester!' Emmy said brightly. 'It's just silly homework stuff for a class project. We're getting ahead of it before the summer's over.' Mrs Winchester didn't look convinced, but she let it go when she spied Porky and Catherine having a hushed conversation just outside, sidling up to the post office doors to have a better listen.

Now that we had invitations ready to send out and posters to hang in the village square, it was time to let everybody know about our Pride day. But, the next morning, when we were ready to put them up, Rita seemed to be one step ahead.

Another notice hung outside the village hall, reading: 'There are to be NO OTHER PUBLIC EVENTS planned this summer that could obstruct the annual fete. Public events may resume once the summer is over, and all must be run through your local authorities.'

'Local authorities?' I said, aghast. 'Isn't that just her?!'

Gran, who'd dragged me and Riley out with her so we could leave Mum to her painting in peace and buy toilet rolls even though she still had a cupboard full of them, snorted to herself, shuffling on by without a second glance. She'd insisted on walking, although I'd ridden in the scooter just in case she got tired. 'Next thing you know, she'll have us reporting for duty in the square at seven a.m. every morning,' she muttered. 'I've half a mind to throw a huge party for everybody in the village, just to see the look on her face.'

Fortunately, Gran didn't notice the look on *my* face, but Riley was eyeing me with suspicion. 'You're up to something,' she murmured behind Gran's back. I tried not to blink under her watch, because obviously blinking or even breathing is a sign of guilt when you're lying. I shrugged and scooted ahead to help Gran, vowing to avoid Riley at all costs, even if I had to get the spare blanket and sleep out under the big tree in Gran's front garden.

'No other public events!' Emmy said, breathless, as she barged through Wendy's front door later that afternoon. 'Did you see the new notice in the square?'

'Yep, we saw it all right,' Robin murmured, his tongue between his teeth as he concentrated on drawing something that looked like a rainbow archway made up of balloons.

'She can't do that! Surely she can't!' Emmy plonked herself down next to me, absentmindedly handing out pastries from the bakery as Harry came in after her with Smudge in tow.

'She can't, but nobody else is going to say anything, are they?' Noah murmured.

I sighed and stood up, then immediately regretted making myself the centre of attention and sat back down again. 'I think it's time,' I said quietly, hoping the others weren't going to drop everything and run. 'We've got the posters, we've got the invites, and we only have a few days left till August the sixth. If we're doing it like we said we are, we have to do it today.'

'Agreed,' Emmy, Robin and Norman said together. Harry nodded.

Noah was sticking pink and blue feathers on to a crown that nobody had agreed to wear yet. He paused, the feather in his hand trembling slightly.

'I guess it's now or never then,' he said, putting the crown aside. 'How are we going to do this?'

It should've been the easiest part of the whole plan. It was literally just pinning up posters, posting invitations through letterboxes. It wasn't difficult. But suddenly it all seemed so real, and the one thing we'd been telling ourselves we could overcome – Rita's fury – was now the fire we didn't want to stoke.

As we shuffled towards the square, it felt like concrete

blocks had formed around my feet, each step more effort than the last. I kept telling myself to keep going, that we weren't doing anything wrong, and that if the worst happened, at least I had Mum, Riley and, most importantly, Gran, to help. But by the time we turned into the square, my stomach had dropped so far down I was almost sure it was in the soles of my feet. The others didn't look so perky either. If anything, we looked like a bunch of rabbits caught in one huge headlight.

'So, uh . . . I guess we just start then,' I said uncertainly, shuffling the pile of posters in my hand this way and that. Noah looked like he might puke.

Nobody moved a muscle, so I decided to go for it first, stepping up to the metal fence that encircled the square and taping a poster to the railings. It fluttered limply but didn't fall off.

ST REGENT'S VALE PRIDE

A COLOURFUL DAY FOR ALL TO ENJOY,
TO HELP CELEBRATE THE LGBTQ+ COMMUNITY!

A DAY THAT PROMISES FUN,
MUSIC AND LOTS OF LAUGHTER.

THE SQUARE WILL BE DECORATED WITH
EVERY COLOUR OF THE RAINBOW
AND WE ENCOURAGE YOU TO
DRESS APPROPRIATELY TO MATCH!

SATURDAY 6 AUGUST 2022!

The end of the rainbow awaits!

There were glittery rainbows and explosions of confetti dotted around the words, which were, of course, the handiwork of Robin. He'd hand-drawn them on every poster, so each one was unique and wonderful in its own way. He'd been super proud of them at the time, but now his hands shook slightly as he stuck a poster to the side of a telephone box.

'What's this?' a woman asked, swinging her shopping bags by her side as she stopped by one of the posters and read it for herself. 'Ohhhhh, what fun!' she exclaimed, her face lighting up with excitement. 'I'll have to dig out one of my best cardigans. If you hand me one or two of those, I'll make sure the rest of my street know about it too.'

She beamed as she took a couple of posters, but her smile quickly disappeared as she seemed to notice something. 'August the sixth? Isn't that the same day as . . .' Her face fell and she almost dropped the posters. She clutched them to her chest and looked over her shoulder. 'You know this is Rita's day, don't you? I'd hate for you to get into trouble.'

'We know,' Emmy said in a small voice. 'We're hoping we can go ahead with it anyway, Mrs Stowford. It's a really important day to our friend here, and it's going to be a lot of fun. If you could just . . . keep the posters, maybe?

And show them to your neighbours to let them know it's happening? Please?'

Mrs Stowford pondered this, still peering all around for signs that we were being watched. She lowered her voice and leaned closer. 'I suppose I can do that, but be careful – when Rita finds out you're doing this, she'll be furious.' Mrs Stowford gathered her shopping bags, placing the posters inside one. 'You're brave, you kids, I'll give you that. But it sounds like a wonderful day – my Natalie would love this.' With a final glance around the square, Mrs Stowford was on her way.

'Well, I guess that's at least one person who's coming,' Noah murmured.

'Two, actually – didn't you hear her say about Natalie!' Emmy chimed in brightly. 'We'll have filled this square out on Saturday; you just watch.'

So, off we went around the square, taping up posters anywhere we could reach. After a while, I started to feel a lot braver, especially when the people we encountered seemed just as excited as Mrs Stowford had been. I began popping into the shops, starting with Porky's butchers, and asked if we could tape a poster up in the window. Some were reluctant, like Catherine in the café who was worried that her rent prices might go up if she was seen helping something that went against Rita's orders, but all of them eventually caved when I brought out the Smudge eyes (honestly, they're such a good trick, I don't know why we humans haven't been doing it this whole time).

'And that's ... all of them!' Robin said, struggling to hold up Harry, who was taping the last corner of a poster to the noticeboard outside the village hall. He gave it a satisfied pat and Robin dropped him back down to the floor again.

'It's basically impossible to miss them,' Emmy mused, looking around at the posters we could see. They really were everywhere, little pages of colour jumping out all over the square.

And in that moment, I felt proud of us. We were really doing it. Harry had had this crazy thought that I'd taken and run a mile with, not even knowing if it was possible. But somehow, with friends, we'd tried to make it work. We were nowhere near the finish line yet – we still had a long way to go and so much to sort out – but it felt like we were well on the way, and that made me prouder than anything.

CRASH!

The doors of the village hall burst open, almost splintering against the brick, and Rita exploded out of them. She flew down the steps like a wolf ready to bite our heads off, charging right for us. She looked furious. Worse than furious. If she'd grown another head and body altogether, it wouldn't have been enough to contain the fury spilling out of her like toxic fumes.

'HOW! DARE! YOU!' Her mouth was contorted into a snarl Dozer would have been proud of, the words fixed into the shape of her rage and piercing every corner of the square. 'YOU THINK YOU CAN COME INTO MY VILLAGE AND DO WHATEVER YOU PLEASE? AND RUIN MY FETE? HOW DARE YOU!'

People edged out of the shops to see what all the commotion was about. Even more people flooded out behind her, the remnants of a village hall meeting spilling out on to the street.

'AND I KNOW YOU'VE BEEN ON MY LAND, TOO! I FOUND AN ORANGE SCARF IN ONE OF MY BARNS AND I KNOW IT BELONGS TO ONE OF YOU SNOT-NOSED WEASELS!' There was only one of us here who'd wear a knitted accessory in such a loud colour. Noah's hand shot up to his neck, horror dawning on his face. 'I'LL MAKE SURE YOU PAY FOR EVERY LAST THING YOU'VE DONE!'

'Rita, please, they're just kids,' someone tried to interrupt from behind her. Rita whirled around in a blaze of fury, glaring so ferociously at a middle-aged man with glasses that I was surprised they didn't just splinter on his face.

She turned to face us once more, her rage boiling hot. We were done for. She lowered her voice into a menacing hiss that almost made me wish we hadn't started this whole thing in the first place.

'I *will* get you for this.'

My hands were clammy as she let the words hang in the air between us. Reaching for the noticeboard, she tore down one of the posters, giving it the once over before thrusting it into our faces like we'd never seen it before.

'I want every last one of these taken down. Immediately. There will be no *St Regent's Vale Pride*.' She spat those last words like they were poison. 'You've caused enough trouble around here and I—'

She was cut off by the ominous sound of a small engine tearing through the square at a speed not much faster than a snail. Rita looked over our heads and scowled, and when I turned around, I could see why.

Gran was zipping towards us on her scooter, Riley and Mum by her side. They were glaring at Rita like she might turn to stone if they tried hard enough. Relief pinged through me as I stepped to the side to let them come up beside me. Mum put a protective hand on my shoulder, Riley standing just in front of us with her arms crossed. Gran nudged her scooter forward until the front wheel was centimetres from Rita's foot. She turned off the engine, stood up out of her seat, and shuffled around to face Rita eye to eye. Well, I say eye to eye, but what with Gran being so small, she had to look up to see Rita properly. But that didn't make her any less of an immovable force.

'Rita Ruckus,' she said, and each of those words were dipped in enough fury to drown the flame of Rita's contempt. 'If I recall correctly, I told you to stay away from me and my family. But clearly that message was too complicated for you to understand. Shouting at children who can't defend themselves? Well, now try shouting at me. I dare you.'

Rita hesitated before opening her mouth to speak. Then

she seemed to think better of it and jammed her lips into a thin line. The fury was bottled up in her cheeks – I could see it struggling to explode – but she just straightened up and glared over at me.

'This *ridiculous* thing you have going on will *not* be going ahead and ruining my summer fete. I want the posters taken down. And if I catch any of you pesky kids anywhere near my house, I'll—'

'You'll *what*?' Mum said darkly, taking her hand from my shoulder and stepping up next to Gran. She was much taller and didn't need to look up at Rita when speaking to her. Gran *hmphed* to herself, crossing her arms and nodding her head.

'You might have scared me when I was a child, Rita, but I'll be damned if you scare me now, and I'll be double-damned if you scare either one of my kids.'

'We should do a vote,' a small voice interrupted, and we all turned to look down at Harry, who was holding Smudge in his arms. He blushed under our collective stare, but Emmy wrapped her arm around his shoulder, and he seemed to gain some confidence.

'If the summer fete and Pride are on the same day, then why don't people vote for which one they want?' he said, looking up at Emmy for confirmation that he wasn't just being silly. She thought about it for a second and then turned to the rest of us, shrugging.

'Sounds like a fair idea to me,' she agreed.

'And me,' Robin added, raising his hand to illustrate his point.

'Me three,' I jumped in.

Noah cleared his throat and nodded sharply. 'Me four.'

Rita narrowed her eyes. She was about to say something else, but she was beaten to the punch.

'I think it's only fair. Voting is the democratic way, after all.' Norman sashayed into the mix, a smile on his face.

The people behind Rita, and indeed the rest of the people listening in around the square, began to look at each other, scared to be the first to agree or speak up. Jack the handyman took the leap and nodded, raising his hand like we were in school and saying, 'Yep, sounds fair to me.'

'And to us, too,' Miss Hart and Miss Finch chorused.

'I say give it a vote and see what wins,' Porky said.

'I agree,' Mrs Winchester from the post office echoed.

'It's the only fair way,' chimed in Catherine.

'Well, that's settled then,' said Mr Tim, appearing from behind Rita. 'I'll set up an anonymous box in the library and you can all place your votes. We'll read the result tomorrow afternoon at four p.m., so tell all your friends to vote too. No use in letting your vote go to waste now, is there?'

Rita looked like she was ready to turn every last one of us into smoke but, outnumbered, she had no choice but to agree. With an almost imperceptible nod of her head, she stormed off through the crowd, glaring at each person she laid eyes on like that might win her some votes. One by one, the square started to empty, Mr Tim promising to have the box set up in no time at all. Soon enough, it was just my family and friends left.

'Well, that went well,' Norman said, grinning. 'Looks like I missed the opening fireworks, though. Such a shame!'

Gran gave Norman a gentle slap on the arm, beaming up at him. 'I've missed seeing you around, Normie,' she said. But soon enough the smile was gone, and she was looking to me instead. 'Now, what's this event you've been keeping secret all this time?'

Oh yeah . . . that.

CHAPTER 26

SISTERS REUNITED

It wasn't how they were supposed to find out. I mean, I hadn't given much thought to how I'd do it or when, but I supposed I'd imagined that there'd be this big, grand reveal when it came time to tell my family about the Pride plans. So much for that idea.

'So then,' Gran said, turning her attention to me now that the square had emptied. 'Tell me everything.'

Emmy, Noah, Robin and Harry slipped out of earshot, Emmy giving my hand a squeeze as she passed. Mum, Gran and Riley all waited patiently for an explanation as I shifted from one foot to the other, trying to find the right words to tell them about our Pride plan. It almost seemed more difficult than telling Rita, though I couldn't put my finger on why. But I'd already been through so much to get to this point – there was no way I could back down now. I glanced at Riley and took a deep breath.

'Well, I had this idea a while ago that I didn't really think was possible but ... the others all said they'd help because they knew how important it was to me and to ...' I trailed off, my eyes slipping over to Riley. She raised her eyebrows slightly, surprised.

'I just know how much London Pride meant to you and ... well, to all of us really, but especially to you. We had such an amazing time last year when it was the four of us. I've never seen you so happy before. I wanted you to feel like that again – for all of us to feel like that again. I suppose I just wanted us to have the same little bit of happiness we had last year and to make it feel like Dad wasn't really gone, even if it was just for one day.' I dropped my eyes down to the ground, every thought and feeling I'd kept behind that wall beginning to bubble to the surface all at once.

'And, well, it got me thinking ... why not bring Pride here? You know, like that man said on the news. There are Prides everywhere, all around the world. So, why shouldn't there be one in St Regent's Vale too?'

Nobody said anything, and I didn't dare look up

for fear they'd all think I was silly, or that they'd be disappointed in me for causing so much trouble. But, when I counted to five and still not a sound had been made, I risked it and snuck a peek. Riley was biting down on her lip, her cheeks tear-stained. Mum had a hand on her back, and Gran had leaned over to put hers on Mum's and now Mum was reaching out for me and before I knew it, I was crying too. I hadn't realized how much I'd needed to let it out. I'd been so focused on trying to do my best, to keep juggling and not drop a single ball. Because until now I'd always thought that if you pretended you were okay, if you really tried to believe it, then everything would turn out fine in the end. I guess sometimes everybody needs a rock to lean on, even if you think that you don't. Seeing my family holding on to each other now made the wall I'd built up inside myself finally break completely.

'I'm sorry I kept it a secret,' I blubbed through my tears. 'I just wanted it to be a surprise for everyone, and I knew it had to be this weekend, so we could celebrate Dad's anniversary too.'

I'd never seen Gran cry before. She was as tough as they came, the one who'd always kept us afloat when we needed her. But right now, she was fighting back tears of her own as she held on to us all.

'I think you've done something really special. It'll mean a lot to a lot of people,' she said. 'Sometimes, people need to be reminded that they're important too.' Mum nodded, pulling me up into a tight hug like she was never going to let me go.

'I love you, Bumble,' she said into my hair, holding me even tighter. 'Your dad would be so proud. Proud of you both.' She leaned back to look at Riley, who had stood still this entire time with silent tears trickling down her face.

'You did all of this for me?'

I nodded. She didn't say anything. She didn't need to. She crashed into me instead with enough might to knock me back a little. I hugged her back tightly, feeling Mum's arms form a shell around us, and Gran's arms provide the armour on top. In that little cocoon, I'd never felt safer.

'You didn't have to do all of that, you know,' Riley said as we settled down into bed that night. It was already late – later than Gran would ever usually see us out of bed – but we'd stayed up in the living room with Gran's bad game shows and more snacks than we could feast on, laid out on blankets in the living room like a glorious banquet. Now it was way past midnight and a silence, only interrupted by the occasional hoot of a far-off owl, wrapped itself around St Regent's Vale like a lullaby.

'I know I didn't,' I said, slipping under the duvet. 'But I wanted to. I know how much you wanted to go and . . .'

Riley propped herself up on one elbow, an eyebrow raised in question. 'And what?'

I grinned. 'I wanted to go too.'

Riley laughed and threw a cushion across the room at me. 'I knew there had to be an ulterior motive.' She settled back on to her pillow, staring up at the ceiling. 'Do you miss home still?' she mused after a moment.

I thought about it. Of course I did. I missed everything about it. But . . .

'I do miss it. But I didn't realize how much I'd actually like it here, too. I've made friends—'

'And enemies,' Riley butted in, and we both burst out laughing again. Gran gave a pointed cough from downstairs, so we quickly got ourselves back under control and lowered our voices, still giggling in our beds.

'But yeah, I do miss home. And I miss Lucas and all

the plans we had this summer. But this has kind of made me feel like even if we're not home . . .'

'Things will still be okay,' Riley finished, and I nodded because I couldn't have put it any better. Riley pondered that, humming to herself. 'I still really miss home, my friends, Elmina, Taylor.' Maybe Lucas had been right – maybe Riley and Taylor *were* girlfriends after all. 'And I miss Dad too. But you know what, Bumble? I think I agree. Maybe being out here with Gran has done us some good.'

'And you have Ziggy, too,' I added.

'Ugh, I wish I could bring him back to London with us. It's like we've been best friends for years already. He just gets it, what it's like to feel a little different. You know, all my friends back home got it in some ways, but they could never fully be in my shoes because they didn't feel the same way I did. They tried to understand, and they did the best they could, and I love them for it. But sometimes you need to speak to someone else who knows exactly what you mean, even when you're not sure you're making sense. It feels good to know that I'm not on my own.'

Riley smiled to herself, and it filled me with a warmth to see her like that again. 'He seems really cool,' I said.

'Emmy is super nice too, and so are Harry and Smudge. Maybe the whole family are just like that.'

Riley reached out for the lamp and said goodnight, plunging us into pitch black only splintered by fragments of the moonlight. Just as I was drifting off to sleep, one last thing came to me, something I hadn't had the chance to ask Riley in a while.

'Ry?' I said, not sure if I was already half-dreaming.

'Mmm?'

'Colour?'

I was nearly asleep, my last scraps of consciousness slipping away into the night. But I could've sworn I heard Riley's answer.

'All of them,' she said. 'Every last one.'

CHAPTER 27

A VISIT FROM LONDON

'DING-DONG, DING-DONG! I haven't travelled all this way to the back end of nowhere to be left waiting at the door you know!'

I sat bolt upright in bed, still half asleep but more than aware that there must be a criminal at the door because who else would be banging on it in the middle of the night. Except, it wasn't the middle of the night but the middle of the morning and for once, Gran had let us sleep in. Although that still didn't answer my question.

'Morning, Sylvie – I've missed you,' the voice said. 'But I've missed this one even more!' There was a commotion in the hallway, followed by Mum's slightly muffled voice.

But I could tell she was excited and, as sleep started to seep away from me, I quickly realized who it was.

'Riley!' I whisper-yelled, hopping out of bed and more awake than I'd ever been in my life. 'Quick!'

'What's happening?' a sleepy Riley murmured in a daze, emerging from under the duvet and rubbing her eyes with a yawn.

'Downstairs!' I was off out of the bedroom door and thundering down the stairs, bursting into the kitchen to find two people standing there that made me feel like we were home all over again.

'There's the little princess!' Rue screamed, hands to his chest and charging forwards to wrap me up in a hug.

'Nice to see ya, Bumble,' Travis called from the table with a wave. Gran was hurrying around him with a mug of tea and a plate of biscuits.

'And here's the queen, risen from her slumber to grace us with her presence!' Rue spread his arms wide and ran at Riley, who screamed with laughter. 'Good Jesus, Mary and Jackson, I've missed you all!'

'Jackson?' Gran frowned at Rue, who shrugged.

'Terrible date with a Joseph once, Sylvie. Can barely say the name without coming up in a rash.'

Gran laughed to herself. 'Jackson it is, then.'

'So, tell us everything! What's been happening while you've been out here? I want every last detail.' Rue looked at Mum expectantly, who nodded in my direction instead. Rue whirled around, grinning. 'I should've known you'd have been up to something. Come on then, spill. What've you done now?'

Telling Rue and Travis all about the last few weeks and what they'd culminated in was quite possibly the highlight of my life. Rue was as animated as ever, bouncing around all over the kitchen and laughing like an old witch, while Travis gave me a round of applause, the biggest grin on record plastered on his face. I took a bow when I was finished, and everybody clapped.

'Incredible! Are you sure you're not a child of mine? I'll take her off your hands if you ever get tired!' Rue nudged Mum who burst out laughing and gave me a wink. 'So, when's the vote happening? Which we will, of course, win. I was in the scouts back in the day, selling cookies door to door – I know a thing or two about getting people on my side!'

Travis nearly choked on a laugh. 'You went for one day and then cried when you realized you had to walk everywhere.'

Rue stared off into space, a dreamy smile on his face. 'Always was a precious petal, bless me. Anyway, the vote!'

'It's later today,' I said, a small jolt of adrenaline sparking inside me. 'Mr Tim – he runs the library and he's going to count the votes himself.'

'You can bet I'll be there with bells on,' Rue chimed, and Travis nodded next to him. 'If we lose, I'll be the first to throw a brick at the window!'

'Rue!' Mum and Travis scolded together.

'What?! How do you think Pride started in the first place, darling? It wasn't always balloons and confetti, you know!'

Gran got up and started to clear the table, giving Rue a pat on the shoulder as she went. 'I'll be right there with you,' she murmured.

Rue glowed at that. But then he faced us all with a look that meant business. 'Now, serious question – why do I get the horrific feeling there isn't a Starbucks anywhere around here?'

'There is one!' Mum countered. Me and Riley frowned. 'You get in the car and drive to the end of the street. Take a left, then drive some more. And keep on going. Keep on going some more. Until you reach London again.' Rue pouted and muttered while we all burst out laughing. 'Now, if you don't mind, I need to drag these two out to help me with some painting.' Mum tapped Rue and Travis on the shoulder and led them out into the garden, disappearing into the shed.

'What *is* she painting?' Riley wondered, watching from the window as the shed door closed behind them.

'She won't tell us. It's a secret,' I said with a shrug. 'Hopefully it's a poster to help us win some votes this afternoon.'

We were all nervous. So nervous that I couldn't think of anything else but the vote. What if we lost? What if everybody actually hated the idea, or just couldn't bring themselves to go against Rita? What if everything we'd been planning suddenly went down the drain and we never got to have the Pride I'd pinned all my hopes on? I'd seen how happy Riley was the night before, that glimpse of joy we'd missed for almost a year. If we lost now, what would that do to her? To Noah and to Ziggy and all the other people who needed it to happen?

There was something else too, a niggling feeling that

refused to leave me alone. If we didn't win, I'd have let everybody down. Sure, they'd probably tell me otherwise, that it wasn't my fault and that at least I'd tried. But I'd have let them down all the same, and I couldn't bear to think about it. The weight of it sat on my shoulders, as heavy as an anchor mooring a ship out at sea.

At half past three, we all gathered together and started making our way towards the square. As we went, I glanced at Riley out of the corner of my eye. The hoodies she'd been hiding in had been left behind today, proudly replaced with her 'Be Gay, Do Crime' T-shirt, her rainbow badge glinting on the front. Her braids were pulled back out of her face, which was warmed with a soft smile. And that's when I realized that, no matter what happened next, I was starting to get my big sister back, and that was better than anything else I could ask for.

Norman met us outside Dawnlight Cottage, along with Noah and Robin, giving us all a grand wave when he saw us waiting by the garden wall.

'Wait, I know you!' Rue screamed. 'You're that drag queen, aren't you?! Buttercup!'

'DRAG QUEEN! I don't know what you mean, sir,' Norman said with a wink.

We fell into step, Rue talking Norman's ear off the entire way and almost bouncing up into the air with every step he took. Nervous chatter fell between us as we approached the square but I couldn't pay attention to it – my head was all light and dizzy and far away, thinking about everything that could possibly happen next.

And when we arrived in the square itself, I didn't feel much better. It was busier than I'd ever seen it. It was packed with familiar faces: Jack, Catherine, Porky, Miss Hart and Miss Finch, Doctor Dill, Mrs Winchester, even Gran's sworn wheelie bin rival Mr Wittington from across the street, were all there to see how the vote was going to turn out. There was an excited hum of conversation and energy in the air, like a street party that was winding down, or maybe one that was winding up. People nudged their neighbours as we walked by, dropping their heads to whisper behind their hands. I tried to look at the floor, to avoid the watching eyes. But Gran scooted up next to me and tapped me on the arm.

'Head up high, Bumble. You be as proud of yourself as I am.'

Emmy, Harry and Ziggy were waiting for us, standing by two red-haired adults with freckles dotted across their noses and cheeks. I hadn't met Emmy's parents yet, what with their frantic preparation for the summer fete at the bakery, but they both gave me a huge hug and clapped me on the back.

'They want you to win,' Emmy whispered, stepping aside with me and the boys so we were out of the way.

'We all want you to win!' Harry sang, clapping his hands together.

'And we've got your back, either way,' Robin added. 'Whichever way it goes.'

Noah nodded, pointing to an old woman wearing a knitted cardigan with a pink and green diamond pattern on the front. 'My grandma voted for you, so that's one person at least!'

I took them all in, standing around me like they were my shield, ready to go into battle. 'We're all in this together, remember? This isn't just about me, or Riley. It's about all of us.' I put my hand in the middle and the others followed suit, cheering as we threw our hands up in the air. And as Rita came bowling into the square with only minutes to go, irritation flickering around her like a hive of bees, I felt that whichever way this went, I still had my friends by my side. Their support would lift me, regardless of what happened. True friends can make you feel invincible, and I felt lucky to have them.

At exactly four p.m., Mr Tim came scurrying out of the library with a simple box in his hands. He held it with such care and attention, it might have housed a precious jewel or something else equally as expensive. He reached the village hall steps, hopping up them until he looked out over the square. A silence fell. Emmy grabbed my hand and squeezed it tight.

'Hello, hello!' Mr Tim said brightly, holding the box aloft and giving it a shake. 'You've all been voting, and I'm happy to report that every single person in St Regent's Vale has had their say!'

A small cheer bubbled through the crowd. Rita cast her eyes around, her frown so deep that her eyebrows were nearly on her chin.

'I have counted the votes twice, and had them triple-checked by the lovely Ms Latham.' Mr Tim gestured to a young woman standing with her arm entwined with her husband's. She gave a wave to the crowd, the bangles on her wrist jangling together.

'So, without further ado, I guess it's time to reveal the result!' The entire crowd seemed to hold its breath at once, leaning forward as though needing to be closer to hear what was said. 'The vote was very clear in the end – all but a few voted for the winner.'

Mr Tim paused, and I felt like I might explode up into the sky if he made us wait any longer. Noah grabbed my other hand, reaching out for Robin's too, who reached out for Harry's. I glanced over my shoulder to see Riley holding Ziggy's hand, Mum holding on to Rue and Travis, and Gran hanging on to Norman.

Mr Tim cleared his throat. 'The winner of the vote is . . .' I gulped. This was the moment, the one that would decide if we'd been wasting our entire summer on nothing but a dream that couldn't come true. *Please*, I begged nobody in particular. *Let us win.*

There was a moment, a pause that could have been three seconds or days. Then Mr Tim grinned and threw his hands in the air. 'PRIDE! Congratulations to Bea and her merry band of friends!'

We cheered like we'd never cheered for anything else in our lives. I jumped up in the air in celebration, swallowed up by a crowd of people who were celebrating with me. People around the square clapped and hooted, whistled and cheered with us. Every last fear I'd had melted away, banished and replaced with sparks of joy. Relief blossomed inside me, blooming like a beautiful flower.

'You did it, Bea!' Emmy shouted above the noise. 'You did it!'

'YAY, BEA!' Harry yelled, tugging on my arm and jumping up and down as Smudge zoomed around our feet.

Noah wrapped me up in a big hug, the smile on his face brighter than I'd ever seen it before. 'Thank you,' he said in my ear, and I squeezed him back because if I let go, I'd probably float off up into the clouds.

When we broke apart, I looked for Mum and Riley. They were standing hugging each other, watching me. I fought my way through the people between us and fell into them both with relief. For the second time in as many days, I felt myself well up with tears and I didn't even want to stop them. I was just so happy.

'Well, no time for all this celebrating malarky – we have work to do!' Norman clapped. 'This Pride won't put itself together, will it? Dare I say we have some new recruits to help as well?' He looked over at Mum, Rue, Travis, Gran, Riley and Ziggy, who all cheered back. Mr Tim had come down to stand beside them all, his hands clasped together and a small smile touching his eyes.

'I would also like to help, if that's okay with you?' he said.

'And we'd like to help too!' Miss Hart and Miss Finch added in unison, popping up beside Mr Tim.

'Of course,' I said with a smile. 'We'd be happy to have you all.'

As we left the square, skipping and cheering, I looked back over my shoulder, taking in the people still standing around and chatting. And then it dawned on me – all of us had been celebrating the result, but there was one person who definitely wouldn't be. I scanned the faces of everybody in the square, looking for one in particular. But Rita was nowhere to be seen.

CHAPTER 28

A MOMENT FOR NOAH

It was all hands on deck after that, and now that Riley and everybody else were in the loop, we had more hands than ever to help out. There were invitations to be posted, more posters to be hung, balloons to be blown up, flags to be unfurled, banners to be made, confetti cannons to . . . not set off in Wendy's house, which Robin found out the hard way when he twisted one of the tubes and it exploded in his hands, glitter and confetti raining down on everybody.

But even though it was hard and stressful work trying to plan an entire event with only two days left to spare, there was something exciting about it too. There was a buzz, not only in Dawnlight Cottage, but around the whole village itself. The thrill of something new, something fun, hung over the square in the mornings while people popped into shops to grab their groceries; it swept around corners, chasing our tails as we delivered invitations, slipping them into every letterbox we could find; it entwined itself with the breeze, weaving a trail of anticipation and magic in its wake.

As for Rita? Well, she mostly stayed out of the way, locked away inside her big house and apparently refusing to leave it. Someone who'd spotted her in the square early one morning swore blind that he'd seen her rip down a Pride poster, tear it in half, tear the halves in half again and stomp up and down on the remains. Another said they'd spied her burning rainbow flags in her back garden one night. I didn't know how much of this was true, but I couldn't help, in a strange way, feeling . . . bad? I hadn't meant to take over everything or ruin her summer fete, and I didn't want anybody to feel left out.

Which is how I ended up at Rita's house on Friday morning, the day before Pride, an invitation in my hand. I hadn't told the others what I was planning on doing as I knew they'd end up coming with me. I went on my own, not because I was brave but because it felt like the right thing to do.

I forced myself up the driveway and shuffled up the

steps to the front door. With a deep breath, I knocked, fighting the urge to turn and run when I heard Dozer bark. But then Rita's shadow appeared behind the frosted glass window and the door was whipped open. Her eyebrows rose slightly as she saw me before they settled into her usual scowl.

'Come to gloat, have you?' she snapped. She looked thoroughly disgusted by my presence. 'Well, I don't want to hear it. You can all choke on that rainbow as far as I'm concerned.' She lifted her nose in the air and made to shut the door.

'Rita, wait!' I blurted. She hesitated. 'I just wanted to give you this.'

I held out a hand and offered her the envelope. She rolled her eyes, sighing as if this was all a major inconvenience, and snatched it from me, tearing it open and scanning over the invite.

As she did so, I took the opportunity to peer around her into the house beyond. It was old-fashioned and pristine, all polished wood and paintings of like, trees and things. On the dresser in the hallway, there were pictures too. There were snaps of her and Mr Ruckus on holiday together, and also a portrait of Dozer standing tall and mean in the back garden. The last thing I saw before I tore my eyes away was a picture of a much younger Rita and Mr Ruckus holding a smiling toddler between them. It was Norman.

'I said I didn't want to hear any of your gloating,' Rita fumed, peering down at me over the invite with deep suspicion.

'I'm not gloating,' I said, shrugging. 'Pride isn't a place that leaves people out. And if everybody else in St Regent's Vale is invited to come, then you should be too.'

Rita took another look at the invite and then swept her narrowed eyes back over my face, searching for the punchline to a joke she hadn't understood yet. I held my hands up to prove I came in peace. She sniffed and stuffed the invite under her arm.

'Well, as the councillor for this village, I guess I have no *choice* but to be there and keep an eye on the festivities. I'd much rather count grains of sand, but I suppose it's my duty.' She paused, as if she were thinking of some other great insult to throw my way. But, when nothing came to mind, she gave me a stiff nod and shut the door.

As the day wore on, there was an excitement bubbling away in Dawnlight Cottage. Weeks of uncertainty, of wondering if we could do it – *how* we might do it – had led us up to this point, and we were as ready as we could ever be. If we'd forgotten anything, then it was simply too late to get it. It was late afternoon already, the early evening ready to pour itself into the deepening blue sky. I was exhausted but happy, ready to take on whatever tomorrow had to offer.

But first of all, there was something important we had to do. Together.

'Come on, Noah, it'll be fine,' I said encouragingly as we turned the corner on to his street. He'd paused, like there was an invisible fence stopping him from walking any further. Riley patted him on the shoulder and wheeled around so she was facing him.

'You've got this, okay? You can do it.'

'She's your grandma and no matter what you say to her, she should love you all the same,' Norman chimed in. 'You're going to say it and then feel so much freer and lighter and like you're not holding in this big secret. Believe me – we know all about that.' He gestured to Riley and Ziggy, who nodded back.

Noah had asked that we all come with him so he could tell his grandma about what he'd already told me and the rest of us. He didn't want us to come inside, but he wanted to know that we were there.

'I guess I'll see you soon, then,' Noah said, his voice a notch above a whisper. 'You're definitely gonna wait here, right?'

'We're not moving anywhere,' Robin said, and gave Noah a bear hug. 'We'll be waiting right here.'

Noah nodded, more to himself than anyone else, and started up the garden path. He turned when he got to the front door and we all gave him a wave or a thumbs up. He responded with a wobbly smile, opened the door, and slipped inside.

'I hope it goes well for him,' Ziggy said with a sigh.

'It will,' Emmy said, determined. 'Look, there he is!' She pointed at the front window, where Noah and his grandma had just appeared, their backs slightly turned to us.

'I don't know if we should watch . . .' Riley started, but then we saw Noah start talking and even she couldn't help herself.

'Please go okay, please go okay, please go okay,' I

murmured under my breath. I wished it with all my might. Noah had been my first new friend, he'd taken me in and introduced me to the others, so in some way, everything that had happened since was because of his kindness. The thought that this could go wrong, that Noah wouldn't get the reaction he wanted, was enough to make me feel queasy.

Noah appeared to be talking for a really long time. Maybe it wasn't so long, and time just seemed to be going extra slow, but it felt like we were standing out on the street for hours waiting for some sign of good or bad news. Then Noah stopped talking and he and his grandma just looked at each other, unmoving. I held on to Emmy's hand like it was a life jacket in a stormy sea.

And then Noah's grandma moved. She covered the space between them in two strides and the pair of them embraced, wrapping their arms around each other. We all cheered and clapped, hugging each other.

'A happy ending, then!' Ziggy said, jubilant.

'Not quite,' Norman butted in. I looked around us for signs of something gone wrong, but nothing seemed to have changed. 'It's not the end just yet – we've got a Pride to do!'

CHAPTER 29

MUM'S SECRET

I didn't sleep all night. I couldn't. I was filled with nerves from head to toe and my thoughts were running endless laps around my head. It wasn't just nerves either, although that was at least half of it. But the day I'd been dreading for a number of reasons was finally here – Dad's anniversary.

As the first ray of sunlight seeped through the window, I decided enough was enough and got out of bed because sleep surely wasn't coming to me now. But, since it was barely five in the morning, I decided to let Riley rest some more. At least she'd found the respite of sleep.

Unlike every other morning over the past year, now there was this new feeling, one delicately balanced between sadness and hope. Before, it had just been sadness when I woke up and remembered it wasn't a dream and that Dad wasn't here any more. Shaking the sleep away, only to feel the ache that had never really gone away in the first place.

But today, there was hope too. Hope that Dad was still here with us, that we were making him proud, and that we were doing everything we could to keep on going. Because we couldn't stay still, swamped in our sadness. Dad wouldn't want that. In fact, I'm sure he'd have been shouting from wherever he was now, trying to get a message through to us that we were being silly and shouldn't stop living just because he wasn't here any more. Pride had helped to give me that hope, and I planned on having the best day ever in honour of the one person who couldn't be here to experience it for himself.

Padding down the stairs, I was frightened out of my skin when I realized someone was in the kitchen already. It was Mum, floating around the counter, fixing herself a cup of tea. I didn't want to point out the obvious, but it looked like she hadn't had much sleep either.

'Morning, Bumble,' she said as I plopped myself down at the table. 'Couldn't sleep, huh? Me neither.

You okay?' She sat down next to me and observed me properly. She'd been crying, as I knew we'd all do today.

'I'm okay,' I said, and for the first time in for ever, it felt like I wasn't telling a lie. 'It's going to be a weird day, isn't it?'

Mum breathed a gentle sigh, cradling her tea in her hands. 'It *will* be strange. One whole year has gone by. I can't believe it.' She took a wobbly breath and for a minute I thought she might cry. Then she reached out a hand for mine and gave me a smile instead. 'But we'll have each other to see us through the day, and we'll have Pride too. Are you all prepared for it?'

I shrunk back into my chair. 'I think so. I'm just . . . you know, nervous that things won't go the way I imagined them, or that everything will go wrong.'

'And so what if it does? What's the worst that can happen?'

I thought about that, but I couldn't sort any particular image in my head. 'I dunno. I just want the day to be perfect, that's all.'

'Well, a perfect day is one where you're surrounded by the people you love and doing something that makes you happy. Will you have both of those things today?' I nodded without hesitation. 'There you go then. It'll be a perfect day, no matter what.'

Gran hobbled into the kitchen, wincing as she tried to straighten out her back. She fell into a chair as Mum flicked the kettle on again and started preparing a mug. 'I'm gonna have to do some of that yoga business you speak of, Camille, otherwise I won't have a chance in a month of Sundays to shimmy these shoulders later.' Me and Mum laughed.

'You can just do a little shuffle on the spot,' Mum said, setting down a steaming mug on the table. Gran looked horrified.

'These shoulders had the boys swooning back in my day! I'll not be putting shame on this family by doing no shuffle on any spot. You'll be lucky if I'm not spinning on my head on a car roof come midday.' Mum snorted while I tried to make that thought into a mental picture.

For once, Riley rose before eight, slipping into the kitchen and giving each of us a peck on the cheek. Her eyes were glittering with tears as she sat down, but she seemed in a good mood, all things considered. Mum leaned over to give her a hug and a kiss.

'I have something to show you all,' Mum said once breakfast was out of the way. 'I finally finished my painting, just in time for today, and I want you to see it.'

She led the way out into the garden, the sun crawling up the grass and warming everything in its path. It looked like it was going to be a fine St Regent's Vale summer's day. Mum propped open the shed door and dipped inside, waiting for all of us to follow. Her easel was facing the shed wall so we couldn't see what was on it yet, and she stood proudly by its side.

'I didn't know what to paint, but I knew I wanted to make something special for today.' She paused, seemingly searching for words that she couldn't find. 'Well, here goes, I suppose . . .'

She gently placed her hands on the easel, turning it around to face us. We all gasped, my jaw dropping to the floor. It was a portrait, intricate and detailed, with swirls of colour making up a rainbow in the background. Dad looked back at us, an easy smile on his face, like the ones he'd give us when he said 'goodnight' or 'I love you'. It looked so real, I wanted to reach out and touch him.

'It's perfect, Mum,' Riley said, slightly breathless. Gran sniffed and I realized the four of us were crying in the shed.

'If you look a bit closer, it's got a special little detail,' Mum said.

We all huddled in and looked properly. Sure enough, there was a detail that we'd missed. From far away, the rainbow in the background looked like six blocks of colour. But, up close, you could see that each stripe of the rainbow was actually made up of a different name, written impossibly small and repeated over and over again until the rainbow was complete.

Red said Riley.

Orange said Camille.

Yellow said Bea.

Green said Gran.

Blue said Dad.

And purple said Family.

'Now you got me a crying mess before my big dancing number today,' Gran blubbed, and we all laughed through our tears. Coming together, we wrapped our arms around each other, bowing our heads and sending our own private messages out into the world.

I love you, Dad, I thought. *I miss you. I really do. But I can feel you with me, and in some ways it's like you've never left, like you've always been by my side through everything. I hope you're proud of me – proud of all of us. And I hope you stay watching over us for ever.*

CHAPTER 30

THE FIRST PRIDE

At our Pride Headquarters – also known as Dawnlight Cottage – it was like the party had already started. Laughter trailed down the garden path to greet us as we arrived, a dozen voices entwined together. When I opened the front door, Emmy, dressed in a light blue summer dress, flew into me for a hug. The rest of the gang was dressed up for the day too – Robin and Noah were even wearing matching rainbow-striped T-shirts, except Noah had also teamed his with bright yellow shorts and pink socks that were different shades entirely, something Robin had chosen to give a miss. Harry had given Smudge a rainbow collar and ribbons on his ears, which just might've been the cutest thing I'd ever seen.

Standing in the doorway, we all huddled together and did a weird little hug-dance-jump thing to celebrate.

'We're really doing it!' Emmy cried. 'Like, this is *actually* happening!'

'I'M SO EXCITED!' Harry shouted, running off down the hall with arms out to the sides like an aeroplane.

Rue, Travis and Norman were already in the living room, along with Ziggy, who was making a show of flicking his newly dyed purple hair around. They were blowing up even more balloons despite the fact that it now seemed the entire house was actually made of them. Various piles of decorations were scattered everywhere, just waiting to be hung up. Norman was now more than half Buttercup, his face painted and wig firmly in place.

'Anything we can do to help?' Mum asked, scooting up next to Rue and giving him a peck on the cheek.

'Dive on in, there's enough for everybody to be doing something!' Norman sang, shimmying his hips as he started on another balloon.

It was bright and colourful chaos, and I wouldn't have had it any other way. Everything was loud and charged with excitement, creating this bubble around us as we finished the last few bits and started packing things up ready to take into the village.

'Do you think people will actually come?' I asked as we gathered everything up and started checking things off the list.

'Duh!' Robin said, nudging me with his arm. 'Anybody in a hundred-mile radius would be stupid to miss out on this – it's going to be GREAT!'

I really hoped he was right, but there was no going back now either way. Before I knew it, we were out of the door and setting off for the square, everybody holding more than they could reasonably carry, ready to make it look like a rainbow had exploded in St Regent's Vale.

We attached balloons in all colours and shapes to railings. We hid confetti cannon tubes, dozens of them, all around the square, with backups set up on the steps too. We hung Rainbow flags – the ones with the black, brown, pink, white and blue stripes, because according to

Norman, if
we were going to
do this, then we had to
do it properly – in shop windows.

And the hard work everybody had originally
been putting towards the summer fete wasn't wasted
either. Catherine had arranged her jars of jam so that the
colours made a rainbow of their own in the café window.
Miss Hart and Miss Finch had organized their flowers
into a stunning rainbow arch that had been hauled up
on to the steps of the village hall to create our stage.
And Emmy's parents arrived with a carload of cakes and
pastries from the bakery, the biggest of them an eight-
tiered wonder that held Skittles in the middle so when you
cut into the cake, they'd spill out like a rainbow.

A face-painter set up their station in the middle
of the square. And a gigantic banner, which read ST
REGENT'S VALE PRIDE, was hung up high on the
front of the village hall. Someone, somewhere, pressed
play and music started pumping out of speakers that had
been placed all around the square. Little Mix, of course.

I ran around like a headless chicken, helping wherever
I could and making sure everything was as perfect as it

could be. I didn't want a single thing slightly off or out of place if I could help it.

'Oh, Bea, I forgot to mention – I've got some special guests arriving to help,' Norman said as I flew past to help with the banner, which was threatening to fall on someone's head. 'They should be here any minute!'

People started to mill into the square as the morning surged on, browsing the stalls, picking up drinks and food, observing all the decorations, and forming little bubbles to stand and chat in. I couldn't help but feel a huge swell of pride every time I caught someone's face staring around in awe at what they were seeing. I had to admit, things did look a lot different.

And then Norman's guests arrived, and the party really started. A colourful minibus pulled up, parking on the outskirts of the square, and out piled a group of people wearing majestic feathers that reached up to the sky in every colour you could imagine. The word KALEIDOSCOPE was written on the side of the bus and the moment they heard the music, they all cheered and started dancing, sashaying around the square to cheers from the crowd.

'Woooooooow,' Emmy gasped as she caught sight of all the feathers. She was particularly taken with the blue ones, her eyes feasting on all the dancers as they continued to entertain the crowd.

'I think we should get some of those feathers for you,' Noah said, nudging Robin and laughing. 'I think you'd look a picture in those purple ones!' To prove his point, Robin started copying one dancer's moves, but with much less grace and he ended up in a tangled heap.

'Maybe I can try out for them next year after some practice,' he said, grinning.

By the time mid-morning had come and gone, it seemed as if almost everybody in St Regent's Vale was in the square, roaming around and enjoying themselves. Mr Tim had left the library and now sat with Doctor Dill, getting their faces painted together. Miss Hart and Miss Finch were hooting with laughter as they decorated Gran's scooter with tassels. Everybody had a smile on their face. It was just how I'd imagined it.

A beep of horns pierced through the music and din and everybody turned round to see Jack the handyman driving a pickup truck slowly into the square, blaring his horn and waving out of the window. In the back stood Rue and Travis, who'd agreed to a makeover from Norman and now looked like mythical beings crafted out of art and magic.

They waved from the truck bed, holding on to the roof of the car as Jack drove them around the square. The truck itself had been spray-painted in swirls of purple and pink, ST REGENT'S VALE PRIDE tattooed along the side.

Next in our mini-parade was Ziggy, who'd insisted on being a part of the line-up simply because he wanted to show off his purple hair. He grinned and waved from the back of another beaten-up truck that had received a Pride makeover, nudging around the square until it had completed a loop.

There were a few more trucks and vans that followed, including Gran in her newly decorated scooter. She honked her horn and waved to everybody as if she were the queen of the whole village. Based on the reaction from everybody else, maybe she was. But, of course, the best float had been saved for last. And I'm sure you can guess who was aboard.

Norman was in full Buttercup-mode, his tallest red wig towering up into the air, the sparkles on his dress enough to light up a city. He looked more glamorous than I'd ever seen him before. Even the megaphone that he somehow retrieved from the folds of his glittering clothes was bedazzled with gems and rhinestones.

'HELLO AND WELCOME TO THE FIRST EVER ST REGENT'S VALE PRIDE! YES, YOU MAY TAKE PICTURES – I'M HAVING A GREAT HAIR DAY! LOOKING STUNNING, SYLVIA GORDON, THAT CARDIGAN IS DOING WONDERS FOR YOU! AND I— NO, GO AROUND AGAIN, I'M NOT FINISHED YET!'

Norman managed six loops of the square before he was driven away again, to jubilant cheers from the crowd. We'd be lucky if he didn't decide to get back in the truck on the hour, every hour, and complete another dozen loops each time.

The swell of happiness I felt only got bigger when I saw Riley and Ziggy reunite after his appearance in the parade, giving each other big hugs and falling into hysterical laughter at some joke I couldn't hear. Riley looked happy. More than happy, actually. She looked just like she did on that day at London Pride when Dad was there too, when we were there together as a family. It was what I'd wanted all along and, as I watched her dancing with Ziggy without a care in the world, I knew I'd achieved my mission. Seeing my sister light up again made me happier than I even knew was possible. And if I could do this – pull off my secret sunshine project – well, then I could do just about anything.

We caught each other's eyes from across the square. I grinned and she did too, holding up her hands and making a heart shape.

'I love you,' she mouthed, and I nearly burst into tears all over again. Happy tears, though, and that was progress as far as I was concerned.

'I guess it's time for the speeches then,' Noah said, pointing to the village hall steps where Norman had reappeared, standing underneath the rainbow-coloured balloon archway. He gave a wave, and the music was turned down to a quiet hum.

'It's so fantastic to see all of you here celebrating alongside us and proving that no matter how big or small, Pride still matters,' Norman said grandly, and a cheer erupted from the square. He waited for the applause to quieten down before pointing into the crowd, right at me.

'This would never have been possible without one person in particular – a young girl who wanted to put this whole event together, to help celebrate the people she loves and the people she misses.' Norman solemnly bowed his head and my cheeks tingled. 'Pride has always been about acceptance, love, family and friendship, celebrating those of us who came before, and those of us who fight on in their honour. It's about finding ourselves, finding our chosen families, and about finding that feeling of togetherness that reminds us we are not alone. That we have each other.'

Norman paused to gesture around the square. 'It's a colourful day, filled with music and dancing and sparkle and glitter. But we mustn't forget the core values of Pride itself – to fight for the equal rights of those who aren't afforded the humanity they deserve. That we *all* deserve. We should be able to love whoever we love without fear, and nobody should ever have to feel like they are not worthy or valid. Because we are *all* important. Each and every one of us.'

The cheer was deafening as we all erupted into applause, stamping our feet and throwing our hands in the air. Norman put a hand on his chest, over his heart, and bowed his head in thanks. After a good while, when the final clap had been clapped, he stepped aside and gestured for me to come up. My legs suddenly turned to jelly, my heart thundering in my chest.

'You can do it!' Emmy whispered, giving me a gentle nudge towards the steps. The crowd cheered once more as I climbed them. I hoped that I wasn't about to make a complete fool of myself. How could I even follow what Norman had just said? It was perfect.

When I stood under the archway and looked out at the square, I saw just how many people were there. Everybody I loved, everybody who'd ever shown me an ounce of kindness since we got here, and more besides, scattered out all over the street and looking up at me, waiting for me to speak. Mum gave me an encouraging nod, which bolstered my confidence a little. Gran was already dabbing a tissue to her eyes, which she'd retrieved from the sleeve of her cardigan.

'Uh, hi, everyone,' I started, knotting my hands together so they wouldn't just hang awkwardly by my side. 'I don't really know how to follow what Buttercup just said. I didn't really expect all of this to happen when I told my friends I wanted to make our own Pride, but I'm so glad that it did. Before we moved here, me and my sister didn't want to leave our home. I don't think she'll mind me saying this but, um ... well, my sister *really* hated the idea.' There were some chuckles in the crowd. 'But the reason I say that now is because we've been here for a few weeks and we've made new friends – ones that we'll have for ever. We couldn't have done the summer without them. But we also couldn't have done it without each other. Through everything that's happened this summer, we've somehow become even closer as sisters.'

I looked down at Riley, who was nestled into Ziggy and using his top as a tissue. I couldn't decide if Mum was holding Gran up, or if Gran was holding Mum up, but they were holding on to each other for dear life.

'There's one person who couldn't be here today, and he's part of the reason I wanted to make this Pride in the first place.' My voice wobbled but I stood up tall, like Dad would want me to. I wasn't hiding behind a wall any more, and it made me feel free. 'Last year, me and my family took my sister to London Pride and we had the best time. But a few weeks later everything changed. My dad died and our world was flipped upside-down. I don't think we've been the same since. He'd have wanted us to go to Pride again, as a family, and so I hope that, if he's watching and embarrassing us with his dance moves all over again ...' I smiled down at my family. 'Then I hope he's proud.'

'I want to thank everybody for making this whole thing possible and making it even better than I could've ever imagined. So, um, yeah – thank you for coming and I hope you all have the best day ever.'

I hopped down from the stairs and into the arms of my family as everybody who I'd come to know over the summer clapped and cheered once more. Robin, Noah, Emmy and Harry all let off confetti cannons that rained down over us, sparking yet more applause. Someone turned the music back up and people started breaking back off into their own little bubbles, the chatter and dancing returning in full.

'That was beautiful,' Mum said. She leaned in a little closer with a teary smile. 'And he's definitely embarrassing us with his dance moves. He'll be up there doing the robot as we speak.'

When I broke away to hug Riley properly, I saw two people talking through a parting in the crowd. To my surprise, it was Rita and Norman. I hadn't expected her to come, even if she'd said that she would. I had to do a double-take but yep, there was Mr Ruckus standing just behind her, his shoulders bobbing off beat to the music. Seeing Rita and Norman together made every muscle in my body tense up. But they didn't seem to be exchanging cross words – instead, they appeared to be talking about something that was bringing a small smile to Rita's face.

Norman, in his wig, makeup, dress and heels, nodded and smiled back. I didn't know what was being said, and to be fair, it was none of my business. But it looked like something promising, and that was worth celebrating.

As if she sensed me watching, Rita glanced in my direction. Her mask of hatred and rage had gone, replaced with something much calmer instead. We watched each other for a moment as Pride happened all around us and, as she stood next to Buttercup, she gave me a nod of her head. Maybe it meant thank you. Maybe it meant 'you've beat me this time but you'd better watch your back, young lady'. I couldn't be sure, but when she turned away again, I dared to hope that something might have changed in her.

'I can't believe you did it,' Emmy said, appearing by my side and linking her arm through mine. She gazed out over the square with me, taking it all in. 'I've never seen St Regent's Vale like this in my whole life. I wish it could be like this every day.'

'We did it together, remember?' I said, giving her a nudge. 'I couldn't have done it without you guys.'

Emmy's cheeks flushed, a smile spreading from one ear to the other. 'Today's been perfect,' she said, and I couldn't have agreed more.

CHAPTER 31

HOME

'You do promise you'll come back, won't you?'

It was a couple of weeks later and Gran was standing in the kitchen, guarding the door as if she didn't want to let us leave. Out in the hallway, our suitcases were packed once more, filled to the brim and ready to be stowed away in the car. It was almost the end of summer and we were going home. It wasn't going to be the home we'd lived in all our lives – I had to keep reminding myself that wasn't our home any more – but a new one in London. I hadn't seen it for myself yet, but Mum had been to scope it out while she was back in the city for a job interview at an art gallery and had promised it was even better than our last one. It had a bigger garden out at the back with a little shed so Mum could still paint, and it was only a few streets away from our old house, so I wouldn't be far from Lucas. It was going to be a fresh start, something I realized I was looking forward to.

'Of course we'll be back,' Mum said. 'You just try and keep these two away now that they've spent a summer here.'

It was true – after all our whining and complaining, I felt gutted that we were going. Even if it meant finally heading back to London, where Lucas would be waiting to hear about my summer and tell me about his, it meant leaving our memories behind all over again, just like when we moved to St Regent's Vale in the first place. It was ironic, but after so much complaining, a part of me didn't want to go yet. Riley didn't say anything, but I think she felt the same way too. She'd already said goodbye to Ziggy and made him promise he'd come and visit us in London as soon as he could, which he was overjoyed about.

But I still hadn't said my goodbyes yet, and that was the bit I was dreading. 'I'll just be outside,' I said to Mum, who gave me a pat on the shoulder and continued trying to convince Gran that we were going to come back more often.

When I stepped out into the front garden, my friends

were already waiting for me, sitting around on the grass in a scattered circle. I fell into the space between Emmy and Noah, feeling the words I wanted to say – needed to say – clogging up my throat.

'You're *sure* you have to go? Like, *super* sure?' Harry said, trying the Smudge eyes on me. 'You can stay and have my bed if you want.'

I laughed, ruffling Harry's hair. 'I really hate goodbyes,' I started, refusing to look anywhere but at the grass tickling my knees. Tears were racing my words to get out into the world first. I never thought in a million years that I'd make a new bunch of best friends this summer, friends who would be there for me when I needed them most, who would hold me up when I was down. 'This really sucks, but you guys have given me the best summer ever.'

'Us too,' Robin said, and everybody nodded as one. 'You might've even thawed the ice queen herself! I can't believe Rita still hasn't demanded that the Pride decorations be ripped down yet. If I didn't know any better, I'd say she might've even enjoyed it. Who knows, maybe she'll think of doing it again next year too.'

'Okay, let's not get ahead of ourselves. One Pride at a time,' Noah said. He dropped his head a little, murmuring into his lap. 'I know we probably don't compare to your friends back home, but I hope you'll come back and visit us sometime.'

'Hey, don't say that! You can't get rid of me that easily. I'm sorry, but we're friends for life now. You're stuck with me for ever.'

'When do you think you'll come back?' Emmy said, trying to pretend that she hadn't been crying before I came outside.

'Hopefully sooner rather than later. Half term isn't too far away, and Mum's talking about visiting at weekends rather than just saving it for school holidays, so that's something.' I shrugged. 'But you can all come to mine too. It's not very big, and London's all grey and made of concrete, but . . .'

'We'd love to! I've never been to London before!' Noah beamed.

We sat out in the garden for a while longer, reminiscing about summer and making grand plans for the future. The way we were talking, you'd think we were going to take over the world someday. And who knew – maybe one day we would.

With all the suitcases and bags packed into the car,

there was nothing left to do but say our final goodbyes. Norman had already headed back to London, and Rue and Travis were back home too, ready to help us settle into the new house. At least that was something to look forward to.

There was a lot of hugging and maybe a few tears, and by the time we climbed into the car, I felt like I could nap for a hundred years. Goodbyes really are tiring.

'I can't believe we're going already,' Riley said as she buckled up her seatbelt. 'It feels like we've only been here for five minutes.'

Mum heaved a big sigh. 'Just think, this time a few weeks ago, we were all in this car on the way here and . . .' Mum paused, laughing to herself. 'I think we can all agree nobody was very happy about it.' I raised a joking eyebrow in Riley's direction, and she gave an embarrassed grimace. Mum squeezed her knee and grinned. 'What a summer it's been, huh?'

'You can say that again,' I mused.

Mum started the car, patting the steering wheel. 'Give Gran another wave before we set off,' she said.

We started to pull away, up the drive and on to the road. I watched through the back window as Gran, Emmy,

Noah, Robin, Harry, Ziggy and Smudge got smaller. Then we turned another corner and they disappeared from view, as we followed the sun and headed back home, holding on to a summer of memories that we would cherish for ever.

ACKNOWLEDGEMENTS

So it turns out that *book two fears* are a real thing! Writing this book was one of the most difficult things I've ever done and I couldn't be happier that it's finally come together into a story I can be proud of. But I wouldn't have been able to do it without some amazing people in my corner to hold me up, so let me thank them real quick!

First, to my incredible team at Simon & Schuster Children's Books, who continue to be an absolute dream to work with. Amina and Lucy, I'm so lucky to have you as editors and that you not only understand my vision, but work tirelessly to make it the best it can be. I hope you're just as proud of this book as I am. And to Rachel, Ali, Jesse, Eve and the rest of the team – I'll never be able to thank you enough for all that you do. I feel like the luckiest author in the world.

Chloe! You are the best agent I could ever ask for and never bat an eye when I email wild concept ideas that you somehow help turn into books. Thanks for not running a mile when I pop up and say, 'Hey, I know I'm meant to be working on something else, BUT how do you feel about ...' It means the most to always have your support.

Also, a big thank you to my illustrator, Sandhya Prabhat, for once again taking my words and giving them life. I'm always in awe of your work, and I'm so, so lucky I get to have you illustrate my book once again. If I had it my way, we'd hang the cover in the Louvre. I'm working on the petition as we speak.

This book wouldn't exist without my best friends, who encouraged me to keep going even when I asked them to come up with ideas on how to kindly give back my advance because I was absolutely certain I couldn't write another story. Ellen, Ellie, Jack, Matthew, Gena – I don't know what I did to deserve you, but I'm so happy I have you in my life.

Also to Josh, Phil, Kris and Vitor – wild karaoke nights and 'Guys, have you seen this?' texts in the group chat are good for the soul! To my Goslings squad for letting me pick the post-badminton spot for lunch, or letting me moan when I don't get my own way. And to my clique at home (I'm not naming you because you'll enjoy that too much) for all the tennis, pool and movie nights. Thanks for keeping me sane and giving me inspiration for a TV show – I won't kill any of you off in the first episode, promise!

The Secret Sunshine Project is all about family, and it's no coincidence that Bea's foundations sometimes reflect my own. I was raised and loved by strong women who taught me everything I know, and without them, I don't know what I'd do. This book is for my little sister, Ellie, my gran and, most importantly, my mum. I love you endlessly.

And finally, to all the booksellers, teachers, bloggers, reviewers and you, the reader. Writing and publishing my debut book in the middle of a pandemic wasn't quite how I envisioned my dream coming true, but you made it a magical experience all the same. I hope you enjoy it. This one's for you.

BENJAMIN DEAN

© Alex Mayeye

Benjamin Dean is a London-based celebrity reporter. His biggest achievement to date is breaking the news that Rihanna can't wink (she blinks, in case you were wondering). Benjamin can be found on Twitter as @notagainben tweeting about Rihanna and LGBTQ+ culture to his 10,000+ followers. *Me, My Dad and the End of the Rainbow* was his debut book.

SANDHYA PRABHAT

Sandhya Prabhat is an illustrator and animator originally from Chennai, India and currently living in California. She loves illustrating children's books, animated stickers and videos for social media platforms, and for TV and movies. Her work can be seen at www.sandhyaprabhat.com and she can be followed on Instagram @sandhyaprabhat